STOLEN BY TRUTHS

TRUTH OR LIES BOOK 4

ELLA MILES

FREE BOOKS

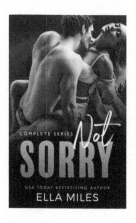

Read **Not Sorry** for **FREE**! And sign up to get my latest releases, updates, and more goodies here→EllaMiles.com/freebooks

Follow me on BookBub to get notified of my new releases and recommendations here→Follow on BookBub Here

Join Ella's Bellas FB group to grab my **FREE** book **Pretend I'm Yours**→Join Ella's Bellas Here

TRUTH OR LIES SERIES

PROLOGUE

KAI

ENZO PROMISED TO PROTECT ME.

He promised to save me at all costs.

To risk his life to keep me alive.

To sacrifice everything to keep me safe.

Enzo promised.

And when Enzo Black promises, he keeps his promise. He never breaks a vow. Never breaks his word.

But sometimes, you don't have a choice.

Sometimes, you can't help but break a promise. No matter how great the promise is—you break it. Not through any fault of your own, but because the world is working against you. Or in this case, the person you are trying to save won't let you save them.

That's what happens when you set someone free. You can no longer control them. No longer protect them. The cage Enzo created for me was safe, but he let me out. And now I'm free to make my own choices even if it risks my life.

I shouldn't be here. I shouldn't be sacrificing everything to keep Enzo safe. But love will do that. I love him. I can't let him get hurt. I can't let him sacrifice himself to protect me.

Enzo made his decision.

I made mine.

And Milo chose.

But Enzo is safe, and to me, that is all that matters.

So that is why I walk willingly into another cage. This cage is beautiful, expensive, grand. Milo's mansion is dripping with wealth. Gold coats the banisters and chandeliers. Valuable and exotic paintings hang on the walls and ceilings like this is the Sistine Chapel or something. And servants stand at attention ready to brush a crumb off Milo's jacket or jump up to lay their life down for him if a bullet were to head his way.

"Come," Milo says.

I stand motionless in the entryway, not believing my eyes. Enzo's home was grand but modern and simple at the same time. Milo's home is a castle in every sense of the word. I'm surprised I didn't have to cross a moat, drawbridge, and dragon to get here.

I force my legs to move again—a difficult task since I don't want to go anywhere Milo Wallace is, and my leg is fractured. The amount of suffering it takes to move is intense. My blood boils with fever with each step, my muscles quiver with weakness, and my bones crunch, further amplifying each break.

But I walk.

I walk to protect Enzo.

Everything I do is for Enzo.

The man I love. A man who is worthy. A man who deserves to be Black.

My arm burns as it falls out of the sling I'm wearing. My shoulder is out of its socket.

I should regret falling in love. Most people at one point in their life or another do. Because the only way you end up with a broken heart is if you fall in love in the first place.

I've had a broken heart. But following Milo now, my heart has healed. Because Enzo isn't the one here suffering. I am. And I can't handle the man I love being in pain.

Maybe I'm stupid for falling in love—especially with a monster.

But I don't care. Because even if I only had a second to enjoy that love, it was worth it. Enzo will always be worth it —always.

I lift my swinging arm and gently put it back into the sling as a drop of blood skirts down my cheek and runs over my lip. The blood tastes cold in my mouth. It tastes bitter and sour.

But my blood saved him.

Enzo may be equally as hurt, but not as damaged. He will get a chance to heal, while I will end up dead.

Not today. Today I will live and wish I was dead. But someday soon, I will breathe my last breath at the hands of Milo.

Milo stops at a door leading down to a basement. His head cocks as a slow grin forms on his face.

I don't want to see what's behind the door, but whatever it is, it won't scare me nearly as much as the man himself does.

"You realize how foolish you are, correct?" he asks.

"Saving the man I love isn't foolish."

He shakes his head. "Falling in love is foolish."

I search Milo's eyes. He's fallen in love before. He wears the same scars I do. He carries his pain as he bears the scar I sliced onto his cheek, like a badge he will never get rid of no matter how much time passes.

"You were once foolish, too," I say.

3

"Yes, and I regret it every day."

"I don't regret falling in love."

His eyes grin at me with all the evil of the world. "You will."

"Open the door, do your worst, I will never regret falling in love with Enzo."

Milo's hand stretches out, and his thick fingers graze my cheek.

I flinch.

Dammit. Don't show fear. Not so soon. Not from the simplest of touches.

"I know everything about you, Kai Miller. I know you can't stand being touched. I know you've endured more pain than most people can survive. And I know you are strong enough to become the true heir of Black.

"I know the more pain I cause you, the stronger you will become. You will turn your body into ice. Your heart into stone. And your mind will block everything out—Enzo included. When I'm finished with you, you won't know what love is anymore. I will bleed you of your weakness until you have none left."

"No," I whisper. He can't. It's not possible. I won't let myself shut down again. I'd rather die and feel everything than give up my love for Enzo.

Milo tucks a strand of hair behind my ear, and I shatter. A low growl of my voice warns Milo to stay away. But instead, it only goads him on.

"We are going to have so much fun together, you and I. I've never had a woman react so strongly to the most comforting of touches."

The only way to protect my heart is to throw up my icy shield and hope if I ever get free, Enzo will be able to crash through my walls once again.

4

"I will take everything from you, Kai Miller. Everything. And when I'm finished with you, you won't have a heart left to give. No love left to protect Enzo with. You will be mine. And together, we will steal the Black empire and rule the world together."

No.

You won't get my heart.

Lock it away.

But the gleam in his eyes tells me that's exactly what he wants me to do. To lock it all away. Because if I do, my love will be gone. I'll become hardened to the world. I'll no longer care about Enzo Black. And Enzo isn't here to break me free. I'll be trapped in my own body with no way out.

Whatever I do, I'm fucked.

My choices are feel everything and hope I'm strong enough to survive it.

Or throw up my shields, lock away my heart, and surrender my love.

Neither option is easy.

But when Milo pushes open the door, I know what I must do. I won't let the devil win. Love wins. Enzo will win. Not by stealing me back, but by keeping this monster from stealing anyone else. I will be Milo's last prisoner. And I will make sure he regrets taking me every fucking day.

1

KAI

ALL I SHOULD FEEL IS pain as I pick up the phone. Instead, all I feel is peace.

I'm free.

Enzo set me free.

But he lied.

He is still trying to protect me. I'm sure Langston is watching me right now in the coffee shop I ducked inside. I order an iced coffee, and then I pull my cell phone from my pocket—the one Enzo gave me. One I'm sure is embedded with a tracking device. Enzo knows exactly where I am, which is why I'll have to ditch the cell phone soon, but not until I make the call.

I dial the ten digits I memorized and then wait.

An intense rage rests in my gut, begging me to let it out. I want to yell, scream, and curse. The man who answers is the man who killed Zeke. I stare at the black scrunchie on my wrist as tears threaten in my eyes.

Why did Milo have to kill Zeke? Why? Why? Why?

Why did Zeke have to die?

Why didn't I stop it?

Milo Wallace will pay for Zeke's death. I will make sure of it. But for now, I have another mission. Ensuring Milo chooses me instead of Enzo.

"I've been waiting for your call," Milo answers without a hello.

"Where do you want to meet to make the trade?" I ask.

"I think you owe me something first," he says.

The tiny amount of coffee in my stomach swirls, threatening to come back up at the sound of his voice. If this is how my body reacts to his voice, *how am I going to react when I see him in person? When he touches me? Hurts me?*

"I don't owe you anything," I hiss into the phone.

"I almost died. Before I make any deal with you, you must apologize to me."

"If you expect me to apologize, then you must really not want to do this deal with me. I'm hanging up now," I threaten.

"Wait," he growls hungrily into the phone. His voice is filled with want and desire.

And the coffee that was in my stomach burns its way back into my throat. *I can't do this.* I need to hang up and find another way to save Enzo. To keep the Black empire safe from Milo. To keep our enemies from touching us.

I don't speak; my throat is like lava. But I don't hang up either. Milo knows I won't. I'm too desperate to save Enzo. I'll do anything he wants.

"I'll text you the address. I'll meet you in the VIP room," he says.

"Time?"

"Midnight."

My feelings overwhelm me, vibrating and trembling through every cell in my body. Fear, rage, love, pain all crash together into a force inside me that whirls through my blood. It's too much. *All of it.* But I won't let the feelings go. I won't lock them away even though it will be easier for me to do what I must. Because despite all the painful feelings, the love shines through the brightest, even if that love is what will be the end of me.

"Don't be late," I purr into the phone, trying to keep my strength and power in this situation. *And don't take Enzo's deal first,* I want to add but don't.

"I think you better worry about your own timeliness, Miss Miller. I'm not the one who will lose if you show up late. You will. And I'll make sure you suffer for your mistake."

"I won't be late."

He laughs. "So much confidence and determination to die, Miss Miller."

"I won't be the one who dies," I threaten back.

"And I won't be the one who sacrifices my life to save another. Midnight, Miss Miller. Not a second late or you know what will happen. You will apologize for all the pain you have caused me. And I will enjoy taking everything from you. So I would think long and hard before you show up, Kai. Because when I'm done with you, even your name will sound like a curse. You will hate everything and everyone. Death will seem more than a blessing. One I will never grant. Not until death seems like the worst choice again."

The phone goes silent.

Rage.

Rage wins out through all the other emotions.

Rage for what Milo did to Zeke.

Rage at him threatening Enzo.

Rage at him taking me.

I may give Milo my life, but it doesn't mean he gets to win. I will not give up that easily.

But first things first, I need to make sure Milo takes me and not Enzo.

———

I SHOW up at the address long before midnight.

I could have spent my last hours of freedom enjoying them. Spending them on a beach, drinking until I'm so drunk my troubles seem like nothing. I would be numb when I finally showed up to see Milo.

But I did none of those things. All I could think about was Enzo. *What was he doing? Did he return to his house by the sea? Is he still on his yacht? Did he try to intercept Milo and make his own agreement? Am I too late? Is he watching me?*

My thoughts also drifted to the naughtier side. My lips yearned to feel the scruff of his face on mine as he kissed my lips, neck, breasts, stomach. My toes tingled thinking of how his tongue feels between my legs. My body ached for his cock to drive inside me.

All things I will never feel again—not from Enzo Black.

Not being with Enzo is ripping me apart. My body only feels whole when he's inside me. When his tongue darts inside my mouth caressing my tongue, when our sweat mixes and our bodies collide in sweet euphoria. Only then am I strong enough to face the world. His touch is the only one I not only can stand but want more of. His grin is the only one I try to earn from a man. His words are the only ones I care to hear.

It may not be healthy to care so much about one man, but I do. Love will do that to you. Make you lose sight of everything else.

But it also feels like more than love.

I stand in a dark alley staring at the club I will enter

closer to midnight. This feels like my destiny. Like I was born to save Enzo and also the entire Black empire. Enzo is the one who can build the empire. He is the one who can grow it to provide jobs for thousands. He is the one who can protect our allies. He is the one who can defeat enemies like Milo.

Keeping Enzo alive and leading the Black empire is more than just my love for him; it's about protecting people who know nothing of the darkness of the world. Enzo's father may not have cared about innocent people, but Enzo does. He may not like to show his heart often, but I've seen it. I know how he cares about the innocent. I know how he cares about protecting those who do not deserve to die. And I know if he were to earn the crown of Black, he would spend the rest of his life protecting those who deserve his protection. Just as he did for Liesel, and he's strived to do for me.

I glance at my phone. It's ten o'clock—two hours until midnight. Two hours I must wait and endure the panic that beats wildly in my chest, threatening to drive me as far away from this place as possible.

I play with the black scrunchie on my wrist—the last thing Zeke gave me before he died.

I wish you were here, Zeke. You would know what to do. You would give me the courage to do what must be done.

I close my eyes, forcing the tears back. If I start crying now, I'll never stop. I didn't even know Zeke's last name. I didn't know his story. I didn't know the woman he loved. I hardly knew anything about Zeke. But I did know he was kind, a gentle giant. I knew his heart was purer than most. We had a connection that in some ways triumphed over my link with Enzo. Zeke and I shared a bond that was so different from anything else I've had before—friendship.

Zeke was a true friend. One who loved me despite my flaws and protected me fiercely.

The wind blows, and I close my eyes, pretending its Zeke's arms wrapping around me, providing me strength. *I'm going to need you with me to survive the next few hours, Zeke.*

When I open my eyes, it seems Zeke sent me more than strength—he sent Enzo.

I watch as he drives his Ferrari up in front of the club. He tosses the valet the keys as he steps out and starts walking to the club entrance.

No.

He can't be here.

He can't give up his life and empire for me.

I won't let him.

I have to stop him.

"Black," I yell from the darkness of the alleyway.

He stops, turning slowly as if he heard the voice of a ghost. But I'm no ghost, just a woman whose voice he never thought he'd hear again. Even though the night is dark, the moonlight barely providing enough light for us to see each other—we see everything. The blackness of the night isn't enough to blind us.

I can see his eyes that were glazed over with determination, soften into tight balls of lust as he sees me. His lips tighten, and his throat closes at the sight of me as if he can't decide whether he is pleased or angry that I'm here.

I feel much the same. My heart races, begging to run and jump into his arms and forget what I must do, while my brain is pissed. He's here when he should be locked away at home where it's safe so that tomorrow he can form a plan to once again grow strong and protect the world from dark men like Milo Wallace.

The valet drives his car away, leaving Enzo and me to stand in the moonlit night. We don't speak, but our bodies say enough—*come here so I can fuck you.* Our eyes say more —*get the fuck away before Milo finds you.*

Stay so I can fuck you. Leave so I know you will be safe.

Neither of us will leave without convincing from the other. And our hearts won't stop until we've had each other.

But for a second, I think Enzo is going to walk inside. He might think that would be enough to keep me outside, but I will never give up. Not as long as I love him. He doesn't realize how much pain it would cause me to know the devil took him while I remained free. I wouldn't really be free if Enzo was caged. I would be in my own personal hell. And maybe after he hears the truth, he will let me save him.

Enzo must realize that ignoring me and walking inside won't stop me. Or the pull we share overrides any rational thoughts he has, because instead of heading inside, he walks toward me.

We don't speak when Enzo stops a step away from me in the dark alley. Close enough to reach out and touch, but far enough away I can't feel the heat from his breath.

Neither of us has to tell each other why we are here. We both know. To make a deal with Milo Wallace. To protect the other person. To sacrifice our life for love.

Neither of us has ever said we love the other. My feelings are strong; I love Enzo in broad daylight even though I have yet to say the words to him. He knows my feelings. Everyone knows.

But Enzo doesn't broadcast his feelings. Most people would say how he acts is love, but I know better. He isn't capable of love. His father broke him of that ability long ago.

Still love is why we are here, and love is why we will both lose everything.

I open my mouth to speak first. I have to be careful with my words because this will be my only chance to keep Enzo from Milo's grasp.

But Enzo's mouth comes down on mine before I get a single syllable out. It's a hungry kiss that feels as much as an attack as a kiss. Our teeth clash as if we haven't been kissing each other every day for months now. Our lips devour each other, and our tongues do battle in our mouths, yelling at each other with our angry pants instead of our words.

His hand tangles in my hair, pulling hard as his fingers fist into the long strands, jerking my head back so he can look me in the eyes.

"Dammit, stingray," he says, using the nickname Zeke gave me.

"Don't you dare!" He doesn't get to use Zeke to get me to do what he wants. "Keep Zeke out of this."

"I can't. Just like you can't. I will use whatever means necessary to keep you safe."

I shove him hard and watch him stumble into the brick wall. Not because of my strength, but because he wants me to attack. He wants me emotional and out of control. He wants me vulnerable so he can persuade me to run and live, while he gives everything to Milo.

Enzo doesn't realize the more I open my heart to my emotions, the more my feelings for him will pour out of me. As it is, my love for him eats at my soul, burrowing deeper into my bones until there is nothing left of me but my love for him.

"You should run," he says, but I don't think he's warning me because he thinks I should run from Milo. He's warning me to run from him. Because what he's going to do to me is anything but sweet.

I arch an eyebrow as I lean forward—our bodies close, but not touching. The whirling sensations bounce back and forth between our bodies. Pulling us closer to each other until we all but collide. "You should run," I threaten.

He sucks in a breath like he's breathing every ounce of me in. Like the breath is enough for him.

I smirk. "Got what you needed?"

"Fuck, never." He grabs my neck and pulls me the last inch into his body. My soft body connects with his hard. And I melt into his arms. I've been trying to be brave, trying to do the right thing to save him, but right now, I don't have to do the right thing. I can do the wrong thing—the very wrong, dirty, naughty thing.

His tongue dances in my mouth, exploring like it's been months instead of hours since our last kiss. And my hungry growls at each intrusion prove I'm in the same desperate state as Enzo is.

"Miss me, stingray?"

My eyes flood with emotions each fucking time he calls me stingray.

Dammit.

I bite his lip as punishment for him playing with my emotions.

He chuckles gently, but I know that is the last gentle thing he is going to give me. I can feel his hardening cock pressing into my stomach, matching every other inch of hardness on his body.

He spins us around until my body is against the brick, and he has me trapped between his hips and arms caging me in. His lips come down on mine again, but he stops short of brushing against my lips again.

I whimper, needing him more than I've ever needed him before. My emotions are raw, broken, and out for him to easily pick up on, even if he wasn't already good at reading my feelings.

But I can tell from the dark heat of his eyes, that he needs to talk before he fucks me.

"I let you go. I set you free, and what do you do? You get captured five-seconds after I let you go. Why, stingray?" his voice drops as he says the last words.

I swallow the lump down. "Because I was never truly free. I left part of me behind when you set me free."

My lips come down on his roughly, shutting him up. *Stop talking Enzo, fuck me...and then let me keep you safe.*

This time, the kiss is enough to drag him under the spell I'm already under myself.

His calloused hand darts under my shirt and over my scared stomach. The touch of his warmth sends delicious shivers through my cold body. And I know the simple contact of my skin against his does the same to him.

What I wouldn't give for a bed right now. We are in a dark alleyway. Anyone could walk by and spot us. We won't be getting naked. I won't get to relish every part of his broken, perfect body. I won't get to kiss over every ripple of muscle. I won't get to lay against his chest until our breathing has regulated to each other's. I won't get any of the things that usually comes with sex.

But I will get everything I need—Enzo. I'll get Enzo. Something I never thought I'd have again.

His fingers brush against my nipples. I'm not wearing a bra. I almost never do and the way Enzo looks at me when he realizes it always sends a shot of electricity from where he touches me to my toes.

"What part of yourself did you leave?" Enzo asks, kissing

my neck as he fists my hair, pulling my head back to give him access.

"Mmm," I moan as he thrusts his cock hard against me. I should have worn heels so I could feel his cock against my clit, instead of against my stomach.

Enzo reads my mind as always and lifts me up so his cock can sink between my legs like I need. We are both still wearing jeans, but the fabric separating us doesn't matter. We don't let something as simple as clothing prevent us from being together.

I tangle my hand in his thick dark hair as his rough stubble brushes against my neck, and he continues to kiss me, hoping to pull all my secrets from me. But I only have one secret left, and he can't pull it from me.

"Tell me, stingray," he nibbles on my ear.

"Fuck me, Enzo," I say, ignoring his request.

His eyes look torn between what his cock wants to do and what he needs me to say. But I know which will win, at least for now.

I grab his jeans and undo the button and pull down the zipper. I reach inside and grab his thick cock, hurrying his decision along to stop questioning me and fuck me instead.

He growls as I fist his cock hard in my palm, gripping him harder than I probably should. But the effect is what I was hoping for.

Enzo practically rips my jeans from my body. "You really should wear more dresses. Easier access," he moans.

I chuckle. "I like making you work hard for me."

His thumb flicks against my clit. And I forget any words I was planning on saying. I forget the reason we are in this alleyway in the first place. The zing zipping through my body at the single touch is too much and not enough at the same time.

I hear a car alarm go off in the distance. I hear people talking as they approach where we hide in the dark alleyway as Enzo plays with my clit. He slows as voices approach.

"Don't you dare stop," I whisper, my breathing already getting heavy and wanting.

His tongue licks slowly and torturously over my bottom lip. "I don't plan on stopping."

I feel his cock pushing hard between my legs as he continues stroking my clit with his fingers, pulling my slickness from my body and drenching his waiting and impatient cock between my thighs.

"Don't scream," he whispers into my ear.

And then his cock slides into me, and I'm full to the helm.

I can't help it. I scream out his name.

I hear the voices stop suddenly as if they spotted us in the darkness. I don't care if they see what we are doing. This isn't about them. This is about us.

No, stop heart. There is no us. This is goodbye.

The voices and footsteps hurry off as Enzo pounds into me.

I feel all of him. His hands are gripping my ass, his cock pounding into the perfect spot in my body, and his lips kissing me as we pant everything into each other.

I don't care about the bricks driving into my back with each thrust. I don't care about the people that keep walking by with their eyes cutting to us; they can't see us in the dark. They can only hear the moans of two people so desperate to protect the other that they are willing to give up their life. And I sure as hell don't care that Milo is probably already in the building across the street, waiting for us.

"Why aren't you free?" Enzo pants, somehow able to

form words even though he's fucking me with the desperation of a dying man.

He's not going to let this go. I run my hands down his back to his ass, pulling him deeper inside of me, needing him to focus on this and nothing more. His jeans still cling to his body, and I can feel the metal of his gun, but also something else. More sharp metal—two circles.

If this was any other time, I would think Enzo was planning on being kinky. He hasn't brought a whole lot of toys into the bedroom; we don't need them. He can show me exactly how kinky and dark he is without the toys. But I can read his mind instantly, and I know why he brought handcuffs with him tonight—and they sure as hell aren't to tie Milo up.

But I shut away my thoughts instantly, because I know as easily as I can read his thoughts, he can read mine. So I only let my thoughts break the surface, and I let myself fall into his plan. He wants the truth; I'll give him the truth.

"Truth or lie..." I start as he keeps thrusting inside of me. I should get a medal for being able to get any coherent words out with him driving into me so deliciously, hitting every nerve ending in my body. All I would have to do to come is relax, but I'm not ready to let go of Enzo yet. *I'm not ready.*

"You knew Milo was still alive when you freed me," I finish.

"Truth," he says.

More thrusts, more kisses, more desperation.

"We are both here for the same reason," I say. We are both here to convince Milo to take us and not the other.

"Truth."

His thrusting gets faster and faster. Our breathing is light and heavy and fast. The pounding in my chest is erratic and unstoppable. We are both so close to coming I don't know how we haven't fallen over the cliff and into the sweet release of orgasm yet. The only thing stopping us is how desperately we are holding onto each other. And how much Enzo is dying for my truth.

My mouth needs his for one last moment that doesn't end in betrayal. For one last moment where I'm his.

The kiss is everything it should be. It's wet, and delicious, and sinful. My kiss says everything I'm about to say and everything I'm not.

When he kisses me harder, I whimper louder, pretending the kiss hurts me because I know how Enzo will react. He won't let me suffer a single second of pain.

He spins us around, holding me to him as he slows his thrust. His strong arms hold me up as I reach behind him carefully, and then I drop my truth.

"I love you, Enzo Black."

He doesn't answer with words. He doesn't clarify if it is a truth or lie—*he knows*. He's always known this is my truth. He knows it's why I'm not free. Because a piece of my heart belongs to him. And I will never be able to get it back.

We orgasm together in one powerful moment. The moment is everything. Because for the first time we made love instead of just fucking. And it happened when we were half dressed, standing in a dark and dirty alleyway where people caught glimpses of the moment.

Maybe it should have been in a bed with clean white sheets, champagne, and flowers. But that isn't who we are.

We are dark.

We are dirty.

We are filthy.

We aren't hearts and roses people. I'd always rather be fucked in a bathroom in a moment of passion than in a soft bed. And I will always want the love of my life to be a little bad than a flawless good-doer who has never been wrong.

Because I'm not a good girl, I'm the girl who used to steal to survive. And I'd rather be bad with a man than fall for a good man. Maybe my heart is darker than I thought.

And my heart is going to break with what I'm about to do next. Enzo is still inside me. His release is filling me as his orgasm still escapes him. He didn't wear a condom, and even if I thought I could get pregnant, I wouldn't care. This was too perfect a moment to stop with any barrier between us.

"I love you," I say again, because I know it makes him vulnerable. It makes me vulnerable too. It opens my heart for him and if last time I left a piece, I'm about to give Enzo every-fucking-thing.

I don't expect Enzo to say it back. So I don't wait for him to. Even if he feels that emotion, he would never say it. *He can't.*

And I can't let him sacrifice everything for me.

I need him safe. I love him. Nothing else matters to me. We both decided Milo Wallace couldn't be defeated with guns and weapons and storming men. And despite how strong the Black empire is, when Milo gathers all our enemies to fight, we won't be strong enough to defeat them all at once. And we won't let our men die for our personal drama.

Our empire is vulnerable. And one of us has to save it. One of us has to get to Milo. One of us has to be on the inside, distracting him while the other finds a chink in his armor. One of us has to sacrifice themselves, so the other can win. But isn't that what the fight for Black has always been?

One loses, sacrificing the job so the other can rule.

I kiss Enzo hard, telling him goodbye with my lips, and then I do it. I don't know if I will get away with it before he realizes what I'm doing. But the glaze over his eyes, the heavy breathing of his chest, and his cock still resting inside of me says this is my last chance to save the man I love.

I grab the handcuffs while still kissing him. Then I attach one to his hand and then the other to the metal pipe running up the brick building.

Enzo's eyes fly open when he realizes what I did.

I dig into his pocket, finding the key. I toss it quickly away so he can't force me to give it to him.

And then I slide off his cock.

His dangerous eyes darken, and I see the fear behind them he's masking with anger.

"Stingray," he says softly. "What did you do?"

I take a step back as I pull my jeans up, covering my body. "The same thing you planned on doing—I saved you."

He exhales, and the anger is gone.

"I couldn't let the man I love sacrifice himself to Milo. Don't hate me for this."

He stands like a statue. "I could never hate you."

He still doesn't say he loves me, but it doesn't matter. I know I will never hear those words fall from his lips, but he got to hear them from me. He will get to take my words with him when he finally gets free and finds me gone.

I glance behind me at the club where I will be meeting Milo and giving him everything he's ever wanted. He will have me—a woman that could have been a queen. A woman he thinks he'll be able to use to get the power of Black. Milo will be wrong though; he'll only get my body, never Black. Never Enzo.

And for the first time, I feel no fear at that. Seeing Enzo again assured me I am doing the right thing.

I look back at Enzo. "Thank you for keeping me trapped. Hold onto my heart and keep it safe for me."

"I promise to keep your heart safe."

"Thank you."

His eyes dim. "I promise to keep you safe, Kai."

I swallow hard as what is left of my heart clenches. I shake my head. "Just my heart. Let me protect you for once."

"Never."

I glance at the handcuffs holding him to the building. "It doesn't look like you have much of a choice."

"I always have a choice."

"Then choose my heart. Because if you let Milo take you my heart will belong to him too. And I want my heart safe. I want my love safe. Protect it, always. Promise me."

"I promise to keep your love safe."

I nod. And then I force my legs to walk. I walk backward so I can see Enzo in the night.

"Goodbye, Enzo," I whisper into the night when I can barely see him.

"Goodbye, stingray."

———

I DON'T KNOW how I'm not bawling like a baby when I leave Enzo. It will be the last time I see him. The last time I kiss him. The last time I fuck him. And the first and last time I tell him I love him.

My heart and emotions are raw and out in the open. Probably not the best place for them to be when I'm about to face my greatest enemy. But I think my emotions like this are the only way I'm going to be able to truly do what I need to do next.

I step into the club that is clueless to the darkness that has just entered and is about to take place here. The music is lively and pounding fast, matching the speed of my heart when I was with Enzo only moments before, but now, now I'm steady as a rock. My heart thuds, slow and dependable. And I know I've never been doing the right thing more than I am right now.

I'm not exactly dressed in club attire. My T-shirt, jeans, and boots are not revealing or tight enough. But it's what I need to be wearing when I face Milo.

I'm early, but I don't want to savor my last few minutes of freedom by myself. I don't want to spend my time drinking at the bar pretending I'm going home tonight. I'm here to save Enzo, and that's exactly what I'm going to do.

I walk up to one of the bouncers. "Show me to the VIP section."

His eyes go up and down my body. "And you are?"

"Here to see Milo Wallace."

At the mention of Milo's name, the man changes. "Right this way, Miss Miller."

I didn't tell him my name, but the bouncer must have been told about me. I follow him through the crowded tables. I glance over at the dance floor where people are grinding and sweaty, oblivious to me and what I'm about to do. *I'm saving them too.* If it were up to Milo, he would take every woman in this club for himself. He'd torture and rape them. I'm giving myself, so he won't do it to them.

I expect to go down into a dark cave, but instead, we go up. The nameless bouncer leads me up a flight of stairs to the VIP room, but it's more like a floor than a room. And the floor opens up to the club below. It's private and not, at the same time. I could scream for help, and as long as I was louder than the music below, people could hear me. It seems risky for Milo, but I know it isn't. He knows I'm going to give myself to him willingly.

"You're early," comes Milo's voice as I step onto the floor.

"I didn't want you to think I wouldn't show up."

He chuckles and stares at me as if he knows a secret— my truth. I showed up early so Milo would take me before Enzo found a way to break free and stopped this.

"Search her," Milo says from his throne of a chair he is sitting on. The two men flanking him approach me and as much as I don't want to be touched; I hold out my hands and stare straight ahead at Milo.

The men run their hands all over my body, searching for weapons. They will find none but the sharp shards of what is left of my heart I plan on using to stab Milo in his sleep.

I tense at their touch. Unwelcome touch still feels like knives being shoved into my skin. But I don't show my pain. I won't let myself whimper, retreat, or shed a tear—no weakness.

The men step away satisfied. And Milo's eyes turn darker. He can't read me as well as Enzo can, but I must have shown some look of pain at their touch as much as I tried not to, because he smiles at the torture running through my body.

"Take a seat," he says as the two men disappear, leaving us alone.

I don't want to follow his orders. I don't want to sit. I want to run. But I won't let myself. I will follow orders until he takes me back to Italy. Until I know Enzo is safe. Only then will I fight back.

I take a seat on the large couch opposite Milo.

"Good girl," he says like I'm a dog.

"When do we leave?" I ask, wanting to get out of here and protect Enzo as soon as possible. I threw the key down a gutter. The phone reception around the club is spotty. It should take him a while to get free from the handcuffs, but I don't want this to linger. I want this done.

"In a hurry?"

"No, I just want the deal finished."

He shakes his head. "You can't save him. Even if I take your deal, eventually I will get him."

I growl. "No, you won't. It's part of the deal. If you choose me, then you leave Enzo alone."

"Who says I've chosen you over him?" Milo asks.

"I have. I'm here; he isn't. I'm the only option you have."

Milo's eyes drift up, and a slow evil grin plasters on his face. And I already know who is standing behind me —Enzo.

I turn and see his dark twinkling eyes burning with a fiery gaze at me.

Fuck.

2

ENZO

WHEN I WALK into the room, Kai's heartbeat, breath, and life stop. The devastation on her face at seeing me here will stay with me forever. She thought she had won when she hand-cuffed me to that pipe. She thought she played me and finally won. And she probably would have if I wasn't so determined to keep her safe.

Langston was nearby. I made sure he came with me to help me stop Kai from going with Milo. If it came down to it and Milo tried to take her, Langston and I would have fought his entire army just the two of us. There is no way Milo is taking Kai from me.

I made a promise to her that I would always protect her.

I made a promise to Zeke's memory that I would never let another hurt her.

I will break neither promise.

So I called Langston, and he set me free. And now I'm here, ensuring Kai doesn't throw her life away to keep me safe. I don't deserve her sacrifice. She's an angel; I'm a demon. If anyone deserves to go to hell, it's me.

"Let her go so you and I can talk, Wallace," I say, but still staring at the woman on the couch. *How could it be that only minutes ago my cock was filling her, her mouth was devouring mine, and her legs wrapped around my waist?* I thought that was happiness, but then she declared her love for me, and I realized what happiness really is. Happiness is being loved by another. Happiness is realizing your feelings are the same. Happiness is forgetting the rest of the world exists.

But I'm not happy anymore—I'm pissed.

Kai outsmarted me. She used my horny cock against me. And then used handcuffs, meant to keep her safe, on me.

I stare unblinking at her as I pour all the words I can never tell her into her body.

You won round one. But you won't win this round. This round is mine.

PS—I love you.

God, I'm in so much trouble. I no longer want to save Kai because I made some twisted promise to her. I want to save her because I'm selfish—because I love her.

"Nah, I think she is going to stay. You both are," Milo says.

My head snaps in his direction. Milo Wallace sits alone. He doesn't have any other men with him, but he had his guard pat me down when I entered. His man found and took my gun, but none of my knives. I could attack now and kill Milo before any of his men got here. But that would put Kai at risk and wouldn't really solve any problems.

Milo's successor would take over his empire. Milo's allies he's gathered would attack. And we would fight a battle we aren't prepared for. When we fight, we need the strength of our allies on our side. We need to understand everything about Milo and his organization. And Kai needs to be somewhere safe, so what happened with Zeke won't happen again.

It takes everything in me not to charge Milo. If it were just me, I would have already attacked. I would have avenged Zeke's death. I would have risked everything, but I won't risk Kai—not now.

I block out the emotions Kai is screaming out without saying a word to me. *Jesus, I can feel every fucking emotion she feels.* I can hear her silent screams for me to turn around and run in the other direction. And I can feel every bit of the torment circling her heart.

Instead, I walk over to her couch and take a seat. I kick my leg up onto my knee and lean back, resting my arms on the back of the couch. I act like I'm sitting down to watch a football game instead of to negotiate with a man I plan on killing as soon as I find a way to keep Kai safe.

Milo chuckles, glancing back and forth between the two of us. "You both are pathetic."

I narrow my eyes. I don't care if he calls me pathetic, but don't push it when it comes to Kai. She is the beauty of the world. She is everything magical, sparkling like the only diamond in a world of coal.

"You are fools, and soon I'm going to show the world just how weak the Black name is. When I take your empire from you, I won't just rule it; I will watch as it crumples until no one remembers how great the Black empire used to be. You used to have the largest domain, with the most employees, most riches, and best technology. You ruled with fear, but now, no one will cower before you."

"Ruling with fear didn't make the Black empire great; it made it weak. Ruling fair with compassion, like Enzo has done, actually earns the respect of the men you rule over. They are loyal to him to a fault. No one would ever turn on him. No one would ever follow you, no matter if you took the empire or not. They would all rebel," Kai says.

But it just makes Milo happier to see her defending me.

"I guess we will see. But first, I must decide how. Which should I choose?" Milo looks back and forth between the two of us, acting like he hasn't already chosen who he is going to pick. *He has. And he will pick me.*

I've never been so sure of something in my life. Milo likes pussy. He likes fucking. He likes raping and mutilating and hurting women. But he can get that easily. He will take me because it gives him the best chance of the empire. And then, once he has me and my empire, he will try to take Kai. Too bad he'll be long dead before it comes to that.

"I want the strongest, of course, the one most likely to win your silly game to become the heir," Milo says.

"That's me," Kai and I both say at the same time. Not because either of us thinks we are stronger than the other, but because neither of us wants the other to get hurt.

Milo laughs. "You two are both so eager to die to save the other."

I watch the wheels turn in his sick, twisted mind.

"Let's make this more interesting. Let's play some games. The winner gets a one-way ticket to my home," Milo says, his dark stare deepening. "I want the strongest, and the only way to determine the strongest is by competing. Best of five rounds wins."

I like games—at least, I like Kai and I's truth or lies game. But after having to compete with Kai in the most fucked up game of all that our fathers created, I don't want to play another game again, especially not one created by a monster like Milo.

"Fine," I say agreeing. I won't show weakness to Milo.

Kai's eyes grow determined as she looks at me. She's going to give this game everything she has.

"Excellent," Milo says, standing up and walking over to

Kai. "Now, for quite a while, I thought you were the strongest, my beautiful Kai." Milo extends his hand to her, waiting and taunting her to take it.

I stiffen, forcing myself not to react and make this worse for Kai. But I can't.

I growl and launch myself over, swatting Milo's hand away. "Don't. Touch. Her."

Milo chuckles in his annoying way, like this is all just a game to him. Like he isn't playing with our lives. Like he isn't playing with his own life. Because everything he does to me, I will do in return.

"Take my hand, sweetheart. Prove you can overcome your little weakness. It's just my hand." Milo leans down and whispers, but I hear every fucking word. "Prove to me if I take you, you can handle my touch, because you will be touching a lot more than just my hand. My cock is going to own every inch of you. Every hole. Prove to me I should choose you."

I snap.

I start for Milo, no longer caring I'm going to have to fight my way out of this club and will most likely get shot, leaving Kai no protection.

Kai realizes I'm losing it and grabs Milo's hand without hesitation or pain. Like my almost outburst pushed away the pain.

Stop fucking saving me, I tell Kai with my mind.

Kai nods, telling me she's okay as Milo helps her up like she can't possibly be able to stand on her own.

Kai may not realize it yet, but she's already lost. Milo will take me. He's just playing with us now. Seeing how strong our feelings are for each other. And then when he's driven the knife deep into both our hearts will he drive the dagger deeper into one of us, while ripping it out of the other.

Milo pulls her to his body as he sniffs her hair. "How is it you always smell like the sea, Kai?"

Milo sweeps her hair over to one side of her neck, and there is no missing the amount of pain on her face at the gesture.

Stay; she's got this. She doesn't need your help.

"Remove your hand," Kai says.

Milo does the opposite. He grabs her hips and jerks her body to his until I'm sure she can feel any erection he has on her ass.

I'm going to kill him.

I jump off the couch like my ass is on fire.

But Kai grabs Milo's balls and from the twisted, white look on his face, I know she's torturing him as he tried to torment her.

"If you want to touch me, you have to agree to a deal with me. Otherwise, keep your hands off me, and I'll do the same to you. Understood?" Kai says.

Milo tries to fight through the pain and act like she isn't hurting him, but her grip is strong.

I fold my arms across my chest as I smile watching the exchange. I never thought I'd be happy seeing Kai touch another man's balls. But this makes me happy.

Milo nods, and she releases him. The hunger in his gaze is undeniable as he watches Kai walk away from him. It's the same feeling I have all the time when I'm around her. And maybe it was a mistake letting Kai handle Milo—he saw her strength in that moment—how fucking incredible she is. How she will fight for everything. How if he takes her, she won't let him touch him without a daily battle.

Fuck, fuck, fuck.

If Milo takes her, I will die. I won't let it happen. He needs to want me, not her. He needs to think I'm the only way to get the Black empire. Even though after the first two rounds of our game, I know Kai is equally capable of running the company.

No, he'll choose me. He thinks I'm his best chance of winning. But it won't stop him from regretting his decision when he's alone with his dick in his hand.

"Let's get these stupid games over with. What's the first one?" I growl as Kai composes herself again while maintaining her adorable glare.

Milo looks at Kai like he wants to get payback. *I hate that look.*

"Strength. Let's see who is physically stronger." Milo devours Kai with his stare that says he both wants her and she is a pathetic weakling at the same time. It's not a smart move on his part. If he thought her grabbing his balls was as bad as it could get, then he's an idiot. She'll find a way to castrate him and watch him slowly bleed out and die.

"Arm wrestle," he says with a wicked grin.

I roll my eyes. This isn't a fair fight, and he knows it. "If you want me to win so badly, just take my deal and move on with it. Don't play these stupid games with us."

Kai clenches her teeth, determined not to let that happen.

Milo pouts his lips. "Kai has a chance to win, if she's strong enough."

Kai walks over to the table, stomping as she walks, clearly pissed she is going to lose the first game without a chance at winning. She puts her hand on the table. "Let's go," she says to me.

I walk over and put my elbow on the table. And then I wait for our hands to connect.

She holds her hand in the air just over mine, excited and terrified of what will happen when we touch. Fucking in the alleyway was supposed to be our goodbye, but it won't be—this twisted game will be.

Our eyes lock, and I wait for her to move the final millimeter. After Milo touched her without her permission, I don't dare force my touch on her now, even though I know she would welcome it. She needs to feel some bit of control.

She wraps her hand around mine, and it's like a shot right to my balls. The tingling from our touch always shocks me. No single touch should feel this fucking incredible.

I suck in a breath relishing this feeling. How her tiny hand feels in my large one.

Milo walks over to the table standing between us. Will there always be someone between us? If we ever figure out how to kill him and take down his entire empire and allies, will there always be something between us?

"Three...two...one...go," Milo says.

I tighten my grip on Kai's hand, feeling her much weaker hand push against mine. But we both know her thin muscles have nothing compared to my bulky bicep. I could win this in two seconds. But I don't want to. I want to feel her hand in mine for as long as possible.

Milo laughs. "Maybe you aren't as strong as I thought, Enzo."

I don't let him taunt me.

Kai looks at me with large puppy dog eyes, begging me to let her win. I would. I want to put Milo in his place and let him know Kai is plenty strong. Sure, her muscles are smaller than mine, but her heart is more than strong enough to make up for any lack in muscle size. And the games for Black aren't like this game. Physical strength isn't the most important factor.

I want to give in to Kai. I always want to give in to her. I want to give her the world. But I can't let her win this. I don't know what other twisted game Milo has in mind, but I need to win this as fast as possible. Milo will not get Kai.

So I suck in a breath, warning her with my gaze, and then I push her hand down onto the table.

Milo chuckles again. "I guess I was right. Enzo is the true heir. But let's play another game to be sure."

Kai swallows hard as she stares at me, still gripping my hand. Pleading with me to not do this. To let her win. She loves me; she should be the one that sacrifices herself.

I can't.

I can't lose you. I love you too. I just can't tell you that.

"What's the next game?" Kai asks.

Milo pretends to think as a waitress comes up and brings him a drink so he can more thoroughly enjoy watching us fight like gladiators to be taken and eventually killed by a man we both hate.

"Speed. Touch the wall ten times and back. The first one to finish wins," Milo answers.

Again, not a fair fight and he knows it. But I don't care. I just want this over. Rip the bandaid off and force me away from Kai. Because the longer this drags on, the harder it is for both of us.

We both walk to the far wall and touch it with our hand.

"Go," Milo says.

We start running with everything we have. Kai is fast, but I'm faster.

Ten turns we run, and I'm thankful this game is something that involves my lungs burning. Running always gives me time to clear my head, and this time is no different. I take the last turn and head to the final wall, with Kai far behind.

I touch the wall easily, breathing heavily. Kai stops in her tracks, panting quickly herself as she grips her knees. She gave everything she had to the game, but it wasn't enough.

Our eyes meet again, and I see the pain and desperation there. Two wins down, one more and it's over. *One more and I win.*

"What's the final game?" I pant.

"So sure you are going to win?" Milo looks to Kai. "But then your competition is nothing but a weak whore, so I guess you should be cocky."

I watch as Kai's fists ball, the veins in her arms pop, and her eyes shoot daggers. He just ignited every drop of strength in her body. I have no doubt if we were to redo either of the last two games, she would win.

I try to get Kai's attention, so I can get her to calm down. Remind her that me winning is for the best. But she doesn't look at me. She's still in a stare-down with Milo.

"What is the final game?" I repeat.

"Strategy, bluffing, and a little bit of luck. You will play one hand of poker; the winner wins the third game," he says.

Fuck. One hand of poker is more about luck than anything else. It involves very little strategy or bluffing.

Milo snaps his fingers, and one of his men come out carrying a deck of cards. We all take a seat around the table, and Milo starts shuffling. He knew the games all along. And even though it feels like just the three of us out here, his men are watching.

I smirk. It's not just his men who are watching.

Milo starts dealing and Kai still won't look at me. She's too focused on winning, on begging the cards to give her a winning hand.

I look down at my hand—three aces, a nine, and a six.

It's a strong hand.

I indicate I want to keep my cards.

Kai glances up at me, looking at me for the first time, and she knows my hand is strong. It's almost like Milo purposefully dealt me a strong hand. She's about to lose.

She returns all of her cards for five new ones.

There is no reason to bet, you either win it all or lose it all. There is no strategy, no bluffing. It's all luck of the cards.

I win with my three of a kind. I know it.

I flop my five cards over, delivering the blow to Kai quickly.

When she sees the cards, she exhales all the oxygen in her lungs.

And then she sadly turns her cards over. A flush. She wins.

Fuck.

I stare at Milo, trying to determine if he helped her win or not. But he just shakes her head not believing it either.

He had planned for me to win three rounds straight. It would hurt her worse to know she was never even a real option for Milo. He likes playing with his food before killing his prey.

Her eyes light up a little bit when she realizes Milo doesn't have another game planned. She threw him for a loop, and that means she has a chance because he doesn't have time to think through his next two games.

"What's next? Squats to test leg strength? Shooting? Stealing? Who can suck your dick better? What?" Kai asks.

And I know he's going to fall for it. She threw in one game she is actually better at along with a bunch of ridiculous games. And his brain isn't working fast enough.

"Thievery. The next game is to see who is better at stealing. The first person to return with a wallet without alerting the person or security to what you are doing wins. And don't even think about trying to leave. My team has the building surrounded," Milo says.

Kai tries to hide the delight in her eyes, but I see it. She could win this game in her sleep.

She starts running down the stairs to the club, and I follow after her.

"That's cheating," I hiss in her ear.

"Oh, really? And I thought this game would be fought fairly what with all the ridiculous strength games. It's clear Milo has no clue the types of games we actually compete in to win Black. You aren't a guaranteed winner just because you are stronger. And if Milo takes you in order to use you to get the Black empire, I will fight harder than I've ever fought before. I won't let him take everything generations of our families have worked to win."

She turns and walks out to the dance floor.

I'm counting on it. If I go with Milo, I want Kai to win. I want her to have all the power of the world. With the army behind her, she can destroy Milo. I'll end up as collateral damage, but it doesn't matter. I thought the best way to protect her was to keep her out of it for so long. But every time I'm around her and get a glimpse of her strength, I realize my own mistake and preconceptions. She might be best off if she wins. She's strong enough to run an empire, and the men who would work for her would take a bullet for her without a second thought because she would make an amazing ruler. And she would earn the men's trust.

Whether she chooses to become Black or not, she will be safe. But I'm not sure if it will be up to her. There are more rules to the game she has yet to discover. And I'm not sure she can meet the final qualification to rule.

I try to focus on my task and find the drunkest person here to try and steal from. Women would be easier to seduce than a man, and then I could steal a wallet, but I don't see a single woman with a wallet or purse on her. I'm sure they all have their money tucked away in their bras, or they didn't bring any money at all knowing a man would pay for it.

Kai spots me scouring the crowd for an easy target. She winks at me, downs her drink, and then bumps into a man in a suit minus the jacket. He's tall, dark, and handsome—every woman's dream. The suit fits him well, his sleeves are rolled up, revealing fit arms, and his hair is still in place despite dancing on the dance floor where countless women have run their hands through his hair. He looks happy and content. If it was me, I would be a sweaty, scowling mess no woman would dare approach.

I can't take my eyes off Kai as she laughs and strokes his bare forearm as she apologizes for running into him.

He asks her if she wants a drink. She nods. And the man leaves, but she turns toward where I'm still standing and starts walking, not waiting for the drink.

She got the wallet. I don't know how, but she did.

Damn her.

She smiles widely, and I follow her back upstairs where we are now tied.

And I know I have to take control if I want to win. I need to win; I don't have a choice.

Kai holds up the wallet to Milo, and his eyes widen.

"That ring you've been searching for, that was me," she says as she tosses the wallet to him.

He catches it, still stunned. He got played, and if he's not careful, we both will.

But I can see the wheels turning. For the first time, he

thinks she might be the stronger one. The one who could win the Black empire. Both Kai and I know she's tough enough. It just depends on the remaining games and how badly I want to win, or she does. But Milo doesn't need to know that. He needs to think she has no chance.

"Yes, she's a good thief. But we've already played that game. She won, but it doesn't mean she will win any more, because I know for a fact one of the games left will involve a fight. A battle of sorts, and Kai has no chance of winning," I say.

Milo finally snaps out of his haze as he decides the final game to win everything. His cock may want Kai, but I know he still thinks I'm his best chance at taking Black. He probably thinks once he's the leader of my empire, he will be able to take Kai then. He just has to be patient.

"The last game is a fight," he says.

"How is the winner determined?" Kai asks, without a nervous tone to her voice.

"When one of you surrenders or death," Milo says sitting back in his chair with a grin.

Fuck.

Kai will never surrender.

And I can't kill her.

I can't win.

But the same goes for me.

I won't surrender because it would mean surrendering Kai to Milo.

And Kai won't kill me either.

I frown. If Milo's goal is to lock us in a never-ending battle, then he got his wish.

Kai takes the scrunchie from her wrist that Zeke gave her and uses it to tie her hair up as if she's preparing for a battle. If I could be jealous of a dead man, I would be. I'm not sure she would mourn me in the same way she does Zeke—carrying him with her everywhere. But then Zeke was worthy of that kind of love. I'm not. Kai may love me, but I don't deserve her love.

She's not physically strong enough for a fight with me, but it doesn't mean she will surrender. No matter how much I hurt her. No matter how much I hold her down, she won't surrender from the physical pain. I have to play with her mind. I have to convince her that giving myself to Milo is the best—for us, and for the Black empire.

"No rules?" I ask as I stand watching Kai trying to come up with her own strategy.

"No rules," Milo answer. "Begin."

Kai and I don't move when he initially says to start. It's like two fighters from the same gym being forced into a ring together.

We start circling an imaginary spot on the floor, both staring at each other, trying to read the other person's mind as we walk. But both of us have put up our shield, and both of us already know what the other is thinking.

She charges at me out of nowhere, jumping onto me with all of her force as she grabs for my neck. I catch her as we fall backward to the ground. Her body is light on top of mine, and I like the feeling despite her trying her best to choke me.

She leans down until her face is at my ear as she continues to squeeze.

"I love you. Don't make me lose you. Don't make me watch the man I love being taken away from me. If you want to save me, then surrender. I gave you my heart, protect it, that's how you can save me," she says.

Her words cut through me like a sharp blade to soft

butter. Her words sting because they imply that while she loves me, I don't love her.

Oh, stingray, if you only knew how much I love you.

I let her think she could win for a second more, and then I flip us quickly, throwing my weight on top of her as I squeeze her neck in return. She couldn't speak if she wanted to.

And then I lean down to whisper my own plea in her ear.

"Trust me, stingray. I have a plan. And the only way I can enact the plan is to get captured. I need to be on the inside for it to happen. Trust me; I'll come back to you," I lie through my teeth.

I don't have a plan, at least I don't have a plan to escape. My plan is the same as it's always been—to keep her safe.

I squeeze a little harder, reminding her she is no match physically for me. She won't regain the upper hand unless I want her to, and I won't let her. If she doesn't surrender though, I'll squeeze until she passes out, and then I'll try to convince Milo it's a victory. I'll convince him to take me while she's still passed out on the floor. The choice will be hers. To surrender and watch me leave. Or fight, pass out, and have me ripped from her.

Tears well in her eyes as her face turns a light shade of purple.

I hate myself for this. I hate myself for hurting her.

But I won't let Milo win.

He doesn't get to touch her.

Ever.

A single tear drips from her eye, and I lean down, not caring if Milo sees the gesture, and kiss the salty tear away.

"Trust me," I whisper again. Trust your life to me. I will keep you safe, even if it means I'll die. You will be safe.

42

Langston will ensure your protection from our enemies. And I'll ensure your protection from Milo.

Kai closes her eyes, like it's physically breaking her to do what she's going to do.

Please, do this for me. Save me.

"I surrender," Kai whispers.

My heart heals with her words. Before each second that passed, more fissures and tears were forming—making me more vulnerable than ever before. But now that I know she will be safe, my heart is whole.

I stand up, getting off her as she continues to lie on the floor—shattered.

One breath.

Two.

Three.

That's all she allows herself to hurt. And then she stands up.

"You surrender?" Milo asks, with a sly grin.

"Yes, I surrender," Kai says without looking at me.

Milo looks to me. "Then it looks like you and I have a deal, Black."

I nod and hold out my hand. He takes it, and we shake.

Milo turns to Kai. "I'll see you at the next battle for the Black empire then." Milo looks to me. "Come, we have a lot to discuss, prisoner."

I take a step forward, and Kai loses it. She runs to me and grabs my neck, kissing me with everything she has. Her tongue wastes no time dipping inside mine as she throws her arms around my neck. I feel her sweet tears running down her cheek, and I feel her heart fluttering weakly in her chest, too broken to function properly.

She's safe.

That's all that matters.

I know she can't physically break the kiss. And so I gently put her on her feet as I break the seal of our lips and exhale, "Trust me, stingray."

I take a step back and signal to Langston who immediately darts from his hiding spot in the shadows and grabs her, keeping her from following us.

And then I do something impossible. I turn my back on Kai and follow Milo. And as much as I don't want to admit it, my heart breaks a little. Milo won't hurt me too badly until he's assured I will win the battle to be Black and give the empire to him.

I'll live at least until the games are over, and then I'm sure I'll die a torturous death—but Kai will live. Langston will help her become Black or set her free. And then she'll find a man worthy of her to get married and live her perfect happily ever after with. Something she deserves more than any woman I've met.

Milo leads me out to a back stairwell.

It takes everything inside me not to turn around and tell Kai how much I love her too. This feels like my last chance to tell her. But I know it would break her more. And it would make it harder for her to stay instead of following me.

So I don't, I just follow. But she devastates my heart when I overhear her speak to Langston, who I know has her in a death grip—it's the only way to keep her from following me.

"What's the plan, Langston? Tell me Enzo has a plan that involves him surviving. Tell me he didn't just lie to me," Kai says.

And Langston, ever the truth teller, breaks what is left of Kai's heart. "I can't."

3

KAI

WATCHING ENZO GO, broke me in a way I didn't expect. I thought my heart would break cleanly—a definite crack down the middle. Enzo would take half my heart, and I would get the remains. Neither parts being enough to save either of us but enough to live a half-life. One with less color, but a life all the same.

But that's not how my heart broke. First, it cracked, then it shattered. There wasn't just one crack; there were many. Tiny pieces flaked off, disappearing into every part of my body to cause havoc. My heart swelled with pain, expanding to a ridiculous size in my chest, searching for the cause of my pain. But even that wasn't enough damage to my heart. After the swelling, my heart crushed like a hundred-ton elephant stomped on top of it.

There is no coming back from that. No way I will heal from the crack, shatter, swelling, exploding, and stomping. My heart is permanently broken.

Forever and ever.

I can't go cold again and lock away my feelings. There is nothing left to protect—Enzo destroyed it.

I collapse to the floor in the wake of Enzo leaving.

The tears and sobs start rattling around in my chest, threatening to break free and drown me.

Langston's arms tighten around me again, keeping me from suddenly jumping up and chasing after Enzo and Milo.

I hate Langston.

I hate Milo.

And I hate Enzo for making me suffer like this.

It would have been hard for him if I was taken. But he doesn't love me like I love him—this is soul crushing.

I won't be able to wake up in the morning knowing Enzo is most likely being tortured.

I won't be able to eat without my stomach wrenching, knowing Enzo's stomach is empty.

I won't be able to look at myself in the mirror knowing it should have been me—I should have been taken, not Enzo. I have experience in being a prisoner. I survived just fine, Enzo won't do well in confined places. He won't do well taking orders. He won't do well on his own.

And I will?

Langston tries to pull me up from the floor.

"No, stop! I can't leave him!" I yell.

"Kai...you have to." His arms tighten.

"No!" I fight him off and run toward the door I saw Enzo disappear through.

I hear Langston's footsteps behind me, but he's too slow. I reach the door, throw it open, and race inside and down a long staircase.

My feet tremble as I run, my tears still flood my eyes, and my breath burns in my chest from the emptiness remaining.

I make it down the stairs with Langston on my heels. I'm

either faster than him, or he realizes I need this. I need to see that Enzo is gone.

I run outside, a new chill in the air. The wind whips around the building, striking me hard in the face, and I stop at the deserted street.

Enzo. Is. Gone.

My eyes search the dark alleyway for a car, a human, any sign of Enzo. But I know I will find none.

He's gone.

He's gone.

He's gone...

Thump...Thump...Thump, thump.

My heart pumps weaker.

Science might say no one can die from a broken heart. It's not possible. But I know in this moment it is.

I feel weak. Dizzy. Lost.

My chest has slowed so much I might need a shock to restart it. The cool blood in my body barely registers, slinking through my body like glue instead of water.

This is it.

This is how I die—a broken heart.

Of all the ways I imagined I would die, this was never it. I never pictured this.

I imagined dying at the hands of a madman.

I imagined drowning in the ocean.

I imagined slipping away in agonizing pain.

But never this.

I close my eyes, trying to feel what is left of Enzo in the air, which isn't much. Enzo lives full and unresolved. He can sweep in and explode into the leader he is, taking charge in a way no other man can, and then the next moment he can whoosh away, taking every drop of oxygen in the room with him.

At least the oxygen I need to survive.

My tears stop, my breath eases, my heart slows.

I'm barely here.

I wouldn't call what I feel peaceful—in fact, it feels like something was ripped from me. I feel empty. I feel nothing. I feel numb. Maybe that's as close to peaceful as I can ever hope to get.

Suddenly, I hear the door behind me as Langston steps out. I don't open my eyes. I don't acknowledge his presence. I'll be gone soon. The wind will take away the pain. My heart will stop beating rather than deal with any more pain. I'm done, and there is nothing Langston can do to stop me.

"If you collapse and stop breathing, I'm going to have to perform CPR and Enzo will kill me for touching your lips. So don't do that to me, stingray," Langston says.

Shit.

My heart clenches as he says stingray, and a soft smile graces my lips.

Thank you, Zeke.

Thank you for reminding me I don't get to die. Zeke sacrificed everything so I can live.

Enzo isn't dead yet. Milo won't kill him until he figures out how to use him to take over the Black empire. *I have time.*

I open my eyes and stare at Langston, and for the first time, I see how much pain he is in too. I can see the desperation to stop following Enzo's orders and chase after Enzo right now. The desperation to leave me alone and unprotected so he can put things right.

We both exhale. And make a silent promise to each other to put each other first.

Langston and I may not have shared the connection

Zeke and I had. I may not love him like I do Enzo. But we are all that we have left—just the two of us.

We have both lost everyone we love.

"We will fight. I'm not ready to give up on Enzo yet," Langston says, staring into the starless night.

I nod. "Together then?" I hold out my hand to him.

"Together." He takes my hand.

One of the tiny cracks heals as Langston takes my hand. *Maybe we can fix everything together.*

———

SOME TIME LATER...

THE SUN POURS into the room, searing into my eyes, forcing me awake.

I moan as I lay face down on top of the covers on the bed Enzo and I used to share. Drool slips from my mouth, and my head pounds from the tiny amount of light blinding my eyes.

Sleep...more sleep.

That's all my brain can process.

I don't know what day it is. I don't know what time it is. I can still smell Enzo on the unwashed sheets, the only thing keeping me present instead of drifting back off to dreamland.

Pound.

Pound.

Pound.

What the hell?

I blink a few times, trying to register what that horrid sound is and how to stop it with the least amount of effort.

My head is foggy. My eyes are blurred.

I moan again but don't move. The sound has stopped. I can go back to sleep.

Pound.

Pound.

Pound. Pound.

I moan louder, trying to drown out the sound.

"Jesus, it smells like someone died in here," a woman's voice says, but I can't register whose voice it is.

That's because someone did die in here—me.

Somehow the room gets fucking brighter.

Kill me now.

Another moan as the woman's heels click against the floor. Only this time, I don't think the moan is coming from me.

"Seriously? Take a shower," the woman says.

I feel hands on my body. The hands burn, but I don't have the strength to fight them.

She rolls me over. And my eyes open.

Liesel.

I growl, she shouldn't be here. She's dressed in a tight skirt and buttoned-down shirt. The kind that makes her cleavage pop while still pretending she's a lawyer instead of a whore.

I hate her. I was content without her coming in here and waking me up. Now she'll force me to face the world without Enzo.

"You two look awful," she says.

I kill her with my eyes, since I don't have the strength to do anything else.

Liesel looks down at the floor where I think Langston is sleeping. That's where he's slept the last however nights it's been since Enzo was stolen from me. I've lost track of time and reason.

"Let go of the bottle of whiskey. I think you've had enough," Liesel says reaching down to take the bottle from Langston.

"No," he snaps like a child who is getting his favorite toy taken away.

The scowl on her face as she rips the bottle from his hands is awful. I know she's going to win. She's much more determined to piss us off than we are to defend our right to sulk and drink our sorrows away.

"What are you two doing?" Liesel crosses her arms over her chest, pushing her perky breasts up higher. I can't help but think her boobs are why she wins any cases in court. Men will do anything for boobs like that.

"What the fuck does it look like we are doing? We are drinking until the pain is gone," Langston says, standing up to meet Liesel's glare.

Maybe he isn't as hungover as I am? Because I'm incapable of standing.

Liesel's eyes flick back and forth between us in a disappointing scowl. "Why?"

"Because Enzo is gone, and we can't get him back. We tried. Wherever Milo took him, we can't get to him. There is nothing we can do. Except for fucking drinking and hoping we die before the pain consumes us," I yell.

The room is silent—for a second.

And then Liesel blocks my sunlight with her curvy body. The look on her face says I'm as dead to her as she is to me.

"And what would Enzo do if the roles were reversed?" she asks, her voice short.

I can't look at her.

"That's right, he wouldn't sulk. He would spend every second of every day trying to save you," she says.

"We tried! I'm not strong enough to save him." My tears threaten again. I thought my tears were done after the first week when I cried until my eyes burned and I couldn't force any more tears out. But apparently, my tears were just hiding somewhere because they are back in full force.

"Maybe you aren't strong enough," Liesel says, not holding her words back.

Langston growls.

"You don't get to be pissed off at me; I'm the only one still sober enough to try and fight to get the man we all love back." Liesel stomps to the bathroom, and I hear the sound of water running. Then she returns to me. She looks at Langston. "Get her ass off the bed and into the shower. Don't worry, I made it cold so your precious skin can handle it." She looks at me then back to Langston. "You shower after her, you reek."

Liesel starts stomping to the door, not waiting for us to follow her orders. I don't know how she's functioning. She lost the man she loves, too. I guess because she's lost Enzo so many times. She lost him the moment he told her he couldn't love her, and she's had years to deal with it. I told him I loved him, and he didn't say it back, somehow that makes everything worse.

"I thought you were stronger than me. I thought you might be the one to break through to him. The one he could actually save because you would be strong enough to save him back," Liesel says sadly from the door. "But I was wrong. You don't deserve a man like Enzo."

And then she's gone.

I look over at Langston who looks as hurt as I feel.

Liesel is right. I don't deserve Enzo. I'm not strong

enough. I'm not worthy. But that doesn't mean I get to drink my life away.

Langston doesn't get to either.

None of us are strong enough on our own. But maybe the three of us together are strong enough to find a way out of this. As much as none of us are worthy of his love or protection—Enzo is worth it. He deserves to be saved.

4

ENZO

Milo Wallace can't kill me. At least not until the games are over.

And I don't know if that makes me feel relieved or horrified.

I can't die.

I can't be killed.

But that doesn't mean death isn't my eventual fate.

As soon as the Black empire is legally Wallace's, I'll end up with a bullet between my eyes.

But that is months, possibly years, from now.

Right now, I'd kill for a bullet to end my misery.

I've been separated from Kai Miller for three minutes and thirty-five seconds. I've counted every single one of them. And every single second hurts.

My heart feels like it's been ripped from my body, jabbed with a thousand barbs and forced back into my chest. My lungs long to breathe in the same oxygen as Kai. My palms feel empty without her long black hair to grab, or her breasts to palm. And my cock has shriveled into nothing, knowing he will never again get to sink into her tight pussy. He is closed for shop—indefinitely.

"Tie him up," Milo says to his men as we step outside.

Before I can react, six men jump on me, wrench my arms behind my back and tie them up. Then move to my ankles with a heavy chain between my ankles.

"Is this really necessary? I just fought to *become* your prisoner. I'm not going anywhere. We have an arrangement; I'm not leaving," I say as the last clink of the handcuffs around my ankles locks in place. My shoulders feel tense as they are pulled back at an unusual angle, and my feet already feel heavy with the chains. But the discomfort gives me something to focus on other than the pain of losing Kai. So why I'm arguing with Milo to remove them is beyond me.

"Yes, they are necessary," Milo hisses as he steps right in front of me. He's a large man, a few years younger than me. His hair has grown long to his shoulders, and his blue eyes turn red when he's angry as he is now.

"Don't think you can take me without putting me at a disadvantage?" I challenge. I have enough rage inside me to kill him and his entire team while tied up with no weapon. The only thing preventing me is the fact that killing Milo would only start a war. One that Kai would have to finish and would put her in incredible danger.

I will never hurt her.

So I don't pummel him in the head like I want.

Milo smirks, reading my thoughts. "They are necessary because I want to hurt you. You have no idea how badly I want to destroy you. You have no idea who I truly am. No idea the pain I've been through. You have no idea how hard it was for me to choose you instead of the whore."

I jerk forward, needing to hurt him after calling Kai a whore. But the men pull me back before I can get to Milo.

"You want my empire? You can have it but leave Kai alone," I say.

He grins. "I think I will take both."

Milo steps into the back of one of the black Mercedes lining the street.

I wrench free and run to the car. I slam my head into his window, getting him to lower it enough to hear me. "That wasn't the agreement. You get my empire, not Kai."

Milo snickers. "And I would never go back on our agreement. No man would want to work with me if I did. But once I become Black, our agreement becomes void. I can do whatever I want then."

Fuck.

All the more reason Kai needs to win.

And I need to find a way to kill this bastard.

Before I can respond, I'm dragged away from Milo's car and into the trunk of another car.

The men laugh as the lock me away in darkness, my body bending in an uncomfortable and unnatural way. They think this is torture. They think this is pain. But I've been trained for years by a father who knew what real pain was and injected me with it on a daily basis.

But now thinking back, even that wasn't real pain. Love is pain. Loving Kai is pain. Losing Zeke is pain. Being surrounded by an empire filled with men I consider family is pain. Being cramped into a trunk for hours is nothing.

Stingray is safe. *She's safe.* Langston will ensure she's safe. He will guide her. Help her either become the next Black or get her the hell away from the danger. Nothing else matters.

Kai. Is. Safe.

And now I have to let her go.

I have to let the pain go. I never told Kai I love her. She is the only woman I will ever, or could ever, love. It's only been a few days since recognizing my love for her, but it is enough to know my life is worth living. Before I couldn't imagine why I was ever born. Now I can't imagine why fate would allow me to fall in love with such an incredible woman who deserves so much more.

Time passes slowly in the trunk of the car. My body bounces around, causing bruises to form and the ropes tying my arms back to tighten until the rope is cutting into my skin.

But I don't care. All I think of is Kai. When the trunk opens and I get out, I'll force myself to stop. To stop loving. To stop thinking. To stop caring. My new focus will be on figuring out how to kill Milo without anyone else getting hurt. Because that is all I can do. I surrendered myself. Soon, I will have to play the third round for the Black empire. And I have no choice but to play it like I want to win.

Milo will only let me live if I play to win. And I have no idea if Kai will try to win or not.

The trunk opens before I'm ready, but I made a promise to myself to let Kai go—so I do. I shut out everything but finding Milo's weakness and exploiting it.

I'm pulled from the car without fighting it. I need to save my strength for what is coming. I know Milo won't kill me, but that won't stop him from torturing me. From keeping me from eating or drinking enough. I'm sure I'm about to face plenty of pain.

My feet hit the ground, and I realize where I am: a private airstrip.

"No yacht?" I ask.

Milo appears next to me. "No, we don't have time for a yacht, even though that is both of our preferred means of travel. We need to get back quickly, I've had enough interruptions. And I don't want that girlfriend of yours to decide to try to wrangle up a crew to attack us."

"You don't have to worry about Kai. She won't attack," I say.

Milo shakes his head as we walk toward his private plane. "Even I know that isn't true."

We board the plane, and I'm shoved toward the back of the narrow aisle-way. And then, I'm pushed to the ground, sandwiched between the last chair and a wall behind it.

Milo's crew board the plane while I stay lying on the floor like a dog. The plane takes off within minutes of us boarding, and I know it is going to be one long and uncomfortable flight for me.

At least I'm close enough to Milo and his men that I will be able to listen to every conversation. I hear the familiar sound of whiskey being poured. The conversations will be flowing, and I will be able to hear every word. It's exactly what I need to be able to learn more about Milo's organization.

It's a good plan, except Milo and all of his men speak Italian the entire fucking flight. A language where I only know the words *grazie* and *ciao*.

So at the first opportunity, I break my promise to myself and let my thoughts drift back to Kai.

Where is she?

Did Langston convince her to stay at my beach house?

Did she buy a new condo for herself?

Has she decided she wants to take the Black empire for herself?

Or has she found a new destiny, one not dripping with pain?

That's where my thoughts start, but not where they end. Instead, my mind goes to much dirtier thoughts.

The shape of her mouth when she's screaming my name.

The curve of her hips as they buck into mine.

The swell of her clit as I press between her lips.

The taste of her tongue as I take her breath away.

The grip of her pussy as she tightens around me.

The scent of her hair sprayed with ocean salt.

The strength in her piercing blue-green eyes as she says I love you.

Maybe I'm delusional. Maybe my heart is fucked. But with each second that passes, I feel my mistake grow.

I should have told her the truth. I should have told her my feelings. I should have said the three words that would have brightened her entire world before engulfing it in darkness.

I. Love. You.

Nope, I'm definitely delusional from going without food or water and being stuck in darkness for so long. That's all.

Except it hasn't even been twenty-four hours yet. My mind is still clear, my belly barely twinging. I'm not delusional. I'm not losing my mind. I'm just hung up on the love of my life. And as much as I want to forget about her and leave her behind, protect her from afar, and with time know she will move on with another man, I know that isn't true. It's not how I feel. If Kai was to move on with another guy, I would come for him. Even if I was dead, I would come back and haunt his ass. Because the love we share is a once in a lifetime kind of love. It's not something you can bury or ever move on from. It's the kind where one of us will sacrifice ourself to save the other. The kind of link between us that no distance, person, or time can sever. The kind that is all consuming. The kind that will destroy continents and start wars. The kind that you never get over. Never escape. And never forget.

The plane lands after several hours, forcing my thoughts from Kai back to figuring out a way to take down Milo Wallace.

I'm led off the plane, but I don't see Milo anywhere. I'm thrown into the backseat of a car this time, instead of a trunk, and a hood is tied over my head. I growl, not because of the darkness but because not being able to see will affect my ability to find Milo's weaknesses. I won't know the path to his mansion. I won't know how many guards stand outside or what security system he uses or where the cameras face.

Milo won't let his team remove the hood until I'm locked inside. I know because it is what I would do if I was holding someone prisoner.

By the time the car stops, I'm exhausted from traveling. My arms ache from being tied behind me. My legs feel heavy from the steel weighing them down.

But it doesn't stop my determination to find a way to destroy this man and keep Kai safe.

The hood isn't removed when we stop. Instead, I'm pulled from the car and walked into the house.

I try to make a move to shake the hood off, but the men are prepared for my sudden flailing and hold it firmly on top of my head. I know I won't be feeling the warmth of the sun for a long time.

I counted the turns as we drove from the airport to the house. There are only six turns. But that doesn't do me a lot of good when I don't know which street to turn on.

And I do the same with my steps. Fifteen steps from the doorway before we turn left. Twenty-three steps until we turn right. Four steps until we hit a door. The door is thick and creaky from the force required to open it and the slamming sound it makes when it's shut. Twelve steps down, the fourth and tenth both make creaking noises when stepped on.

I feel the light through the house as I walk until I hit the stairs. Each step gets darker and darker. And once I hit the last step, I know where I am. Underground where there are no windows and no lights on.

I see the glow of light to my right and suspect that one of the men leading me has turned the flash on his phone on to see where we are going.

Eight steps until we stop again. I hear the cling of a key go into a door and then it opens.

My hood is finally removed as I'm pushed inside the cell —one with bars and everything. The floor is made of concrete. There is a toilet in the corner, a tattered mattress with a pillow and thin blanket, and a hose for water in the corner. For most people this would be their hell, but it's nicer than the rooms my father kept me in. It has all the basic necessities.

I step inside, but the ropes and chains aren't removed.

And the door doesn't close. Which means the men are waiting for something. And I have a feeling I know what that is.

I hear the footsteps of his boots. I examine my surroundings for any sort of weapon. But the best weapon is my own boot and the concrete walls and floor. Everything can be used as a weapon. You don't need a knife or gun to take down your enemy. You don't need your hands or feet. You need determination and the will to never give up. No matter how bloodied, beaten, or pained you are. You never give up.

My father drilled that into me so many times I will

never forget it. My body doesn't have a choice but to fight. I don't stop, even if I want to. And Milo Wallace is about to figure out just how big of a mistake it is to step into my cell.

"Leave us," I hear his voice behind me, but I don't turn around. My toes dig into my shoes, gripping them trying to calm myself. I'm supposed to be on Milo's side. I'm supposed to show him how willing I am to do whatever he wants. Instead, I want to murder him.

The men slowly walk up the stairs, and I hear the loud clank of the door shutting and locking as Milo enters.

"You and I have some unfinished business," Milo says.

I don't react. I don't give him any clues of how I'm going to respond. He thinks he has the advantage because my arms are tied behind my back, and my legs are weighed down. He thinks he could easily get me to stop attacking because of the knives on his body or the gun he could aim at my head.

He's wrong.

None of those things will stop me once I start. Only death will stop me.

Closer, closer, closer he steps.

The sound is faint against the concrete, but I know exactly how far behind me he stands. Close enough I could elbow him in the nose and get a quick kick to the groin in before he can recover.

Restraint, I wait. I won't make the first move. But he will. Even though it's not a fair fight. Even though I'm tied up and he's free. Even though he's facing my back instead of my face like a man.

I grin.

Milo is evil. He was taught how to fight by getting the upper hand. I was taught to fight after I had already lost.

He swings, his shadow confirms it as I duck, turning to face him with a cocky glow in my eyes.

He narrows his gaze to hide his surprise in me ducking and missing his first hit.

"You should have kept your goons with you if you wanted to beat me to a pulp," I say, smirking while trying to undo the knots holding my hands together.

Milo just chuckles lightly as he steps forward. He slowly rolls up the sleeves of his white, and most likely expensive, buttoned down shirt. Like rolling the sleeves up are going to prevent his blood from dripping all over it.

"I'm going to enjoy watching you bleed, boy."

I raise an eyebrow. "Boy? Really? What are you? Fifty? I'm at least three years older than you."

"You are going to feel like a boy when I'm through with you." He throws another punch in my direction. This time more precise. Again I duck out of the way before he makes contact.

I see the anger etched in his face. His cheeks redden, the veins in his eyes darken, and the scowl on his face tenses. I know what he's going to do and this time I let him. I don't shy away from physical contact. Not when I know I'll be able to get some good damage back.

He charges at me, wrapping his arms around me as he slams me into the wall behind. My fingers crunch against the concrete, but otherwise, I absorb the impact, keeping my head from hitting the wall. As long as I don't let him get a good head slam into the concrete, I'll win.

"When is the next game?" he pants.

I smile. "Think you are going to cause too much damage I won't be able to fight against Kai?"

He punches me hard in the stomach. I tense my abs, trying to absorb the punch.

"When is it?" he growls.

"I don't know. Archard, the man in charge of running the games, only gives us twenty-four hours notice before the game starts."

Milo huffs, and I take the opportunity to knee him hard in the stomach as payback. It takes a lot of energy to lift my leg as the chains are heavy, but it's well worth the energy when Milo doubles over and releases me.

My eyes seer with pleasure as I kick him again and again. "You should have tied my feet better if you didn't want me to fight back."

Milo takes a step back, trying to catch his breath again. This man may not have had my childhood, but he's dealt with his fair share of blows before. It doesn't take him long to recover.

"What is the next game?" he growls.

So that's what this is. I realize after the second question. He wants answers. He wants assurance that I can give him my empire without him having to fight. And he wants to punish me as he does it.

Fine, I'll enjoy extracting my own blood while we do business. Maybe it will take away from the pain in my chest.

He rams me again, this time my head coming dangerously close to slamming into the concrete wall.

"Don't know. Each of our fathers took turns picking out a game. The next game was created by Kai's father. So it will probably play to her strengths as did the first game," I say, before headbutting him, breaking his nose.

I grin as it sits crooked on his face with blood gushing.

I've had my own nose broken dozens of times. It isn't the most painful place to get hit, but it's always a bruise to the ego since tears almost always come hand in hand with the gush of blood. You can't stop it. The punch is too close to the tear ducts.

I smile wider when I see the tears. "Pussy. You had enough?"

He growls and spits blood out. "You think a broken nose is going to stop me?"

"No, I fucking hope it doesn't, otherwise I'm giving my empire to a pussy."

He runs at me again. I try to side-step him, but he's more nimble since he isn't shackled. He dives for my legs taking me down hard. My head hits the concrete floor causing a gash to my head. But I'm still conscious. Although, I'm sure it's enough for a concussion.

"I'm not sure I picked the strongest after all," he spits as he takes cheap shot after cheap shot to my face.

I growl before using my head against his again, knocking him back.

I don't argue with him about whether he picked the strongest. I may be physically strong, but Kai is strong in a way I will never be. She is worthy. She is strong because she wants to be, not because her father taught her lesson after lesson.

"How many rounds are left?" he asks.

"We are tied one to one, first to three wins. If I win the next two games, I will become Black. I will own the entire empire."

He stands, trying to kick me while I'm down, but I roll and quickly get to my feet.

"How do I know you will then turn your empire to me?"

"The contract Archard sent you. I had to name an heir. It has to be blood-related. Archard confirmed you and I share blood. I think we are long lost cousins or something. He didn't say exactly how. Anyway, my heir has to be younger. One of the next generation, so to speak. So that means I technically made your future child my heir."

He narrows his eyes, not liking my words.

I smirk. "I take it you haven't had a child yet."

"No." He stops punching for a second, taking my words in. "And even if I did, I don't want my child to be the heir. I want to rule."

I nod. "Which is why you are the guardian of the heir until you have a child or one that is old enough to take over."

"So you win, and then you just give me your empire?" he asks.

I crack my neck back and forth, loosening up as if I'm going to the gym and not beating the crap out of this guy.

"Yes and no. When I win, I will be made Black. You need to have a child before that happens. So that child becomes heir. But until that child is old enough, eighteen to be exact, you will be able to rule as his or her guardian."

He frowns.

"You'll have eighteen years to rule or get the rules of the empire changed."

His frown lifts.

But I have one more piece he's forgetting about. And I'm going to enjoy telling him. No matter who he stole, there is still the possibility he will lose it for himself.

"But there is one more thing. The change of rulers only occurs after the current ruler's death."

Milo smiles. "I'll have no problem killing you when this is all over."

I nod. "I know, but then you will have to have your heir compete against Kai's heir for the honor of being Black. At least when the heirs both turn eighteen."

Panic reads over his face even though there is no reason to panic.

"Another battle? You never said anything about another battle! After you win, I thought you could change the rules to make me Black fair and square."

I shrug. "Don't think an heir of yours could win?"

He grabs my throat and shoves me hard against the wall again. I feel the concrete digging into my scalp, slicing through like butter. This time I wince at the pain. I pushed him too far.

"An heir of mine could win."

"Good, because I can't change the most basic rule of how the Black empire runs, especially not in the few hours you are going to allow me to live after I become Black."

He growls.

"Besides, I don't think there will be another battle. I'm not even sure Kai truly has a chance to win this battle in the first place."

He narrows his eyes. "Why not?"

"Because to win, you have to declare a blood heir—either your child or the child of a brother or sister or other direct relation. Kai has no family left other than her father. So that means she would have to have a child herself to make her heir."

Kai has no family left because my family made it their mission to kill any Millers alive. So that this exact situation would eventually happen. So that the Rinaldi's, my family, could claim the title of Black forever. It was a smart plan, except I'm surrendering the title to this madman before me who only shares a single drop of my blood.

Milo tightens his grip on my throat with every word that leaves my mouth. My head is pounding, and my breath is shaky.

"So she'll have a child. I don't understand why this helps me?"

I croak. "Loosen your grip, and I'll tell you."

He reluctantly does.

"Because Kai isn't capable of having a baby. No blood relation, no heir, no throne. You can only become Black if you have a direct relative who is of the next generation. There always has to be another leader ready and waiting to take over your place. To fight to become Black. And there has to be a guardian worthy of taking over as Black that the winner of the game declares."

I can see Milo still doesn't follow everything.

"I win. I become Black. I declare you as my immediate second in case of my untimely death. I make your child my heir. You kill me and become Black. The Miller bloodline ends with Kai. Which means you and your heir become rulers of Black forever."

The bastard grins as he finally understands how he gets my title, my empire, and most likely, my girl.

I smirk. He can think he will get Kai. He won't. I've put enough backup plans in place to ensure that will never happen.

"I can't wait until I get to kill you," Milo says.

"And I can't wait until you join me in hell."

I attack with my full force, driving my bloodied head into his chest, knocking him down hard. And then I don't let up kicking.

He just chuckles though, and I hear the sound of footsteps nearing.

"Really? You truly won't fight fair, will you?" I say getting one final kick in before his men storm the room. Two men restrain me as Milo gets up, spitting out blood.

Milo thinks he can hurt me. He thinks he can do

damage. And I'm sure when he's done, my body is going to be broken and covered in blood. It will be the last time he touches me though before the game. He wants me to be strong enough to fight against Kai and win quickly.

But Milo can't hurt me. My heart belongs to Kai. To the woman who will soon find out the rest of the contract. She will find out she has to birth a child for a chance at winning. Something she knows in her heart she can't do. I hope we are both wrong. I hope she can have a child and have her chance to fight to become Black. Maybe by then I'll be able to find a way to kill this bastard without risking her.

It kills me to think she can't have a child. That choice shouldn't be taken from her by anyone. But not being able to produce an heir might be the one thing that saves her from this world.

5

KAI

"We need to attack now," Liesel says.

"No, we need to wait until the next game. We need to wait to attack," Langston says.

Liesel pouts her lips, sticking out her curvy hip like that is going to convince Langston. "Ever heard of the benefits of a surprise attack?"

Langston gets in her face. "Ever heard that it is over-played and there is no such thing as a surprise when the enemy is expecting us to attack to get our leader back?"

Liesel rolls her eyes. "Every day that Enzo is with Milo is a day he is suffering. A day that will do untold damage to him. He doesn't deserve that. We need to get him back, now!"

Langston puffs his chest. "Enzo is strong. He spent his entire life suffering. I don't think a few days locked in a cell will hurt him."

"He doesn't deserve to have to deal with any suffering! Why don't you realize that?"

"Because the worst that Milo will do to Enzo is lock him in a cage and deny him food. He won't kill him. He won't physically hurt him. Milo needs Enzo in order to take the Black empire. Enzo is safe! Possibly safer than all of us!"

I sigh as Westcott brings us coffee, but I'm hoping he laced it with alcohol because I'm going to need something stronger if I have to keep listening to both of them bicker.

"Will you two stop it?" I snap.

Langston growls.

Liesel huffs.

Their eyes intensely locked on each other. Their breathing hard and fast like they can't decide if they want to kill or fuck each other.

I shake my head. Emotions have been high since Enzo was taken by Milo, but there is something else going on between the two of them. A past I'm not privy to.

"Either fuck each other and get it out of your systems or drop it, but I'm not dealing with you two arguing," I say.

"He's a prick and a manwhore. Just being in the same room with Langston puts me at risk for contracting an STD. I think I'll pass," Liesel says, walking over to the patio chair next to me and taking a seat.

"Like you don't fuck every man with a cock. Don't deny you are begging me to fuck you. You're just uptight because you haven't gotten laid in months after being trapped on that yacht with all of us," Langston growls taking a seat next to me.

"Enough," I warn Langston. I'm putting it on his shoulders to stop the bickering. I know him better than Liesel, and from the limited time I've spent with Langston, I know he's a playboy. One who hasn't gotten laid in a while. I need to make sure they both get laid because I'm afraid if they fuck each other the bickering will get worse, and they won't be able to stop fighting long enough to help me get Enzo back. Langston is used to following orders. He follows Enzo's all the time. He will follow mine.

I take a sip of my iced coffee. I've had two days to try to think of a plan. And I know what my next step is.

"So what are we doing, oh, great leader?" Liesel says snakily.

Don't kill her. You might need her.

"Archard is meeting us here," I say.

"Archard? Why?" Liesel asks.

"Because I need to read the contract between our families. I need to find out exactly how Enzo plans on giving the empire to Milo. What the rules are, so we can figure out what we need to do to stop it from happening. Or at least how we can use it to our advantage to save Enzo."

Liesel and Langston shut up after that, both sipping their own coffees staring into the quickly rising sun while we wait for Archard.

He shows up at nine on the dot.

I stand and greet him. As soon as I turn my back on Liesel and Langston, they are at each other's throats again.

"You just think you are better than me, smarter than me, that's why you want to get your way," Liesel says.

"No, I just don't trust that you actually give a fuck about saving Enzo. There is always another reason why you do what you do," Langston answers.

I tune them out as I greet Archard. "Thank you for coming."

"Of course, that's what I'm here for," Archard answers.

I motion for him to take a seat at the patio table, away from Liesel and Langston. He does and hands me the contracts.

"What did Enzo do before he left? Did he make Milo his heir?" I ask.

"In a way, yes," Archard thumbs through the papers until he gets to the page. "You didn't read every detail at our last meeting, did you?"

I shake my head no.

Archard points to the clause. "Before the final game, each participant must select an heir. The heir must be blood-related and be at least fifteen years younger than the participant. You must also select a guardian of the heir that would lead if you were to die before your heir reached the age of eighteen and were allowed to compete."

"Milo isn't related to Enzo though. And he's not fifteen years younger," I say.

Archard pauses. "Milo is blood-related, but you are right, he's not fifteen years younger. Which is why Milo is only the guardian of the heir. Enzo named Milo's child as his heir."

"Milo has a child?"

"Not to my knowledge, but that doesn't mean he won't have one by the time of the last game."

I nod. So this is how Enzo got Milo to choose him over me. He convinced him he was the stronger one and going to win, then he made Milo and his child his heir.

"Is there any way to change who Enzo's heir is?"

"Enzo can change his heir at any time before the final game."

I nod.

"Have you thought about who your heir will be?"

My heir.

"No, I haven't. Who can I choose from?"

"A close blood relation's child. Or a child of your own."

A child of my own—I both love and hate that I'm incapable of having a child. I want a child more than anything. A chance to start again. A chance to change my family's

74

destiny. But I don't want to bring a child into this dark world. I don't want them to suffer as I did, all for a chance to win an empire. I don't want to have them spend their life preparing to do battle against Milo's heir, which is what it would take to give them a shot at winning. I don't want them to feel the weight of knowing they must win in order to prevent a monster from taking over an organization capable of controlling the world.

The Black empire has access to more security systems and weapons than almost any other organization. If it falls into the wrong hands, then the world could be controlled by a dangerous man. I still don't understand how the world survived with Enzo's father as ruler of the empire. It won't survive if Milo is the ruler.

However, I don't get to make the decision to have a child. My body isn't capable. Maybe it's time I find out for sure though.

"How much time do I have to find or produce an heir?" I ask.

"Until the final game. Round five. The rules state that all five games are played, even if someone has already won three rounds. At that point, you will lock in your heirs and determine the games for the future generation of Black."

"And when will the final Black round take place? If I'm supposed to have a child to be my heir or Milo needs a child to be his heir, don't those children need time to be born?"

"Yes, of course. The final game can wait to be played up to a year after the fourth game. If you both have a living heir after the fourth game is finished, then the game takes place immediately. If not, then you get one year to produce an heir."

That still doesn't give me a lot of time. To either get pregnant myself or find a blood relative with a child.

ELLA MILES

"Thank you, Archard. Any clue as to when the next round will happen?"

"You know I can't give you that info."

"Even if the fate of the Black empire falling into the wrong hands depends on it?" I need time to figure out a plan. I need time to find an heir. I need time to protect Enzo.

Archard scrunches his nose. "I'm sorry, I can't."

And I'm not sure if he would even if he could. I have no idea who has Archard's loyalties, but I doubt that it's me.

I get up from my seat and return to the bickering fools on the other side of the deck.

Liesel's face is now bright red, and Langston has a goofy grin on his face as he stretches his arms behind his head.

I glare at them, and they immediately drop their discussion.

"What did you learn?" Liesel asks.

"That Enzo made any child of Milo's his heir. Apparently, they are blood-related."

Liesel smiles, and her eyes glaze over. "I'm not surprised. Milo is sexy as hell. He has the same tanned skin and dark hair that Enzo has."

I ignore her comment and keep talking.

"In order for me to have a chance at winning and keeping the empire away from Milo, I need to have an heir by the final game."

"Awesome, so who are you going to choose? Me or Langston?" Liesel asks.

I shake my head. "Neither of you are blood-related."

She frowns. "Have any siblings?"

"Nope."

"Cousins?"

"Not that I'm aware of."

"Any long lost child?"

"Nope."

Liesel looks across to Langston, eyeing his crotch. "Well, you better get to work then." She smirks as she says it.

It takes me a minute to catch on to what she is saying. But it catches up to me all at once; she wants Langston to fuck me so I can have a baby.

"Ew, no. No offense, Langston."

"None taken," he says with a grumpy look.

"Besides the fact that Enzo is currently occupied, there is another problem when it comes to me producing an heir."

"What?" Liesel asks.

"I don't think I can have a child."

Silence.

Liesel's mouth falls open a little, and I can see the pain cutting across her perfectly curled eyelashes.

Langston clears his throat, clearly uncomfortable.

Finally, Liesel regains her composure. "I'm sure we can find a far off relation with a child we can make your heir."

I nod. I have to have some relative.

Which gets me thinking, how close of a relative do I have to find to make my heir?

Archard has packed up his things, but he's still standing at attention as if he knows I'll have more questions for him before he leaves.

Slowly, I walk over. I already know the answer in my heart to the question I'm about to ask, although I don't know how it's possible. I don't know how Milo gained the right to his own empire if what I think is true.

How did they grow up on such different continents but somehow end up exactly the same? How did one grow up trained to be evil turn out so good? And one who grew up away from the darkness turn so evil?

"How close of a blood relation does the heir have to be?"

"The child of a sibling, first cousin, aunt, or uncle."

I take a deep breath, not wanting to know the answer to the next question. "How are Milo and Enzo related?"

"They are half brothers."

I close my eyes as if that will block some of the shock from entering my body.

Brothers.

Half-brothers.

"Do they know?" I ask.

"No. Enzo only wanted me to verify that they were blood-related and Milo could be the heir."

I nod slowly as if on reaction.

Enzo has a brother who is evil. Just like his father. And if Milo finds out, he'll be even more hellbent on trying to take over the Black empire. He will feel that he's owed it after growing up without a father.

I feel Langston and Liesel standing behind me, taking the information in.

"If you need anything else, you have my number," Archard says, putting his hat back on and picking up his leather briefcase.

He must read the shock on all of our faces. "I'll give you as much time as I can to figure this out, but you don't have long."

"Thank you," I say.

And then Archard leaves.

I take a deep breath; I don't have time to dwell on the fact that Milo is Enzo's half-brother. It doesn't matter. Not in the grand scheme of things. Just one more way this world is smaller than I realized.

"I need to find an heir to prevent Milo from winning. And I need to find a way to save Enzo. Are you two going to help me or not?" I ask.

"Maybe this is a sign that you shouldn't? That you just need to drop it and go live a long happy life away from all of this," Langston says, his voice broken and dripping with pain. It's not what he wants. He wants me to fight. But I have a feeling Enzo made him vow to do whatever it takes to keep me safe. And trying to convince me not to try to save Enzo in the first place is part of that promise.

"I can't do that," I say.

He nods and smiles slightly. "Good."

"So you will help me?" I ask.

His grin gets bigger as he looks from me to Liesel. "As long as I don't have to take orders from Miss Bossy Britches over there, then yes."

I chuckle as Liesel frowns, obviously not happy but she doesn't verbally object.

"Deal," I say, not giving Liesel a chance to say anything.

"We need to take care of the heir problem first. As much as I want to storm in and save Enzo, I don't think we can. Milo is too smart. And Enzo is safe for now, at least as long as the games last. I need an heir to keep me in the game."

Liesel crosses her arms but doesn't argue with me.

"Let's split up so we can get to the part where we save Enzo faster. Langston, you do an extensive search to see if I have any long lost siblings or relations I don't know about. Even if they are too far away in blood relation, I want to know about them."

"On it," Langston says, running off.

And that leaves me and Liesel. I don't want to say the words. I don't want to go to the doctor. I don't want to know the answers.

"Come on, I'll hold your hand while you go to the doctor to get tests," Liesel says.

I roll my eyes at her sarcasm. "I don't need someone to hold my hand."

"No, you need someone to drag your ass to the doctor and make it happen. Let's go."

I sigh and follow Liesel.

I'm coming Enzo. Don't give up hope. I remember what my life was like after I gave up hope that anyone would come for me. And it destroyed the tiny spark that was left of who I was deep inside. I don't want that fate for Enzo. Too much time is wasted trying to get it back.

Find an heir, then find a way to save Enzo. Should be easy enough.

Except it would be easier to find a needle in a haystack. Because I'm not sure if I will ever get past step one.

6

ENZO

THE FIRST NIGHT I spent as Milo's prisoner was the worst. He and his men beat me until I had no fight left.

My face was smashed in, my nose broken, my lip busted, my eye bulging, and my head rang with a bad concussion. My broken ribs jabbed into my lungs every time I took a breath. Thick, dark bruises and knife gashes covered my body.

Luckily many of those injuries have healed in the two weeks since that night.

Milo is one angry, vindictive man. And he thought one night of torturing me would be enough to soothe his soul. Enough to make me pay for creating an empire bigger and stronger than his.

But one day isn't enough to tame the monster within. He could have asked me that. I know from my own experience with my own demons.

Milo is a smart man though. He knows one day was all he gets. Now he has to be patient. And it turns out, Milo isn't a patient man.

I hear the familiar sounds of the boots coming down the

stairs, and I sit up on the edge of the mattress on the floor to put on my running shoes.

Every day at ten in the morning and seven in the evening I get let out for two hours at a time to train. It's more exercise than I usually get at home. Apparently, Milo thinks if I'm in the best physical shape of my life, I won't have any choice but to win the games. But I don't complain. It makes the time go by faster.

My life since being Milo's prisoner has been relatively easy. I have a comfy bed. I get three nutritious meals a day. Plenty of exercise. And books about war strategy and brain teasers Milo thinks will help keep my mind sharp for the games.

It almost feels like a luxurious vacation if it wasn't for the dark cell, prison guards, and bars holding me in. And the fact that anywhere that Kai isn't is my own personal hell.

The guards reach my cell.

"You going to keep up with me today, Felix?" I ask every day. So far, I've only been allowed to run in the gym. But I'm hoping to convince one of the guards to run outside with me. I want to know everything there is to know about Milo's mansion and security. I want to know so I can destroy him.

Felix shakes his head. "No, but I'll enjoy taking you down during a boxing match."

I smirk. I like Felix. He's loyal but is the only man here who actually talks to me. A man I might be able to persuade to my side.

"You're on," I say as the door unlocks.

I walk to the door, and the other guard who never speaks puts his gun on me.

I chuckle. "You know I won't run, right? If I leave, then Milo has every right to torture and kill my girl. I won't let anything happen to her. Therefore, I will never run. You don't need to point that gun at me." As if a single gun pointed at me would be enough to take me down if I did decide to run.

Felix chuckles with me. "Give Konrad a break. He doesn't understand trustworthy men. He thinks all men are pigs."

I raise an eyebrow as I follow them up the stairs. "Aren't all men pigs?"

He shrugs. "Yes, but some are honest pigs."

We reach the top of the stairs and then freeze.

One of Milo's men is standing in the hallway, but that isn't what is shocking. What is shocking is who he is holding onto—a woman. A woman with a striking resemblance to Kai. A woman who has fear in her eyes, a dark circle under one of them, and a heavy bruise beneath his grasp.

"Gentleman," he says, nodding to our presence. He has an evil grin on his face. "I was just delivering this whore to Milo's rooms. He'll be home in a couple of hours and needs to blow off some steam."

Konrad smiles back, but Felix frowns. He doesn't like his boss' extracurricular activities any more than I do.

We start walking again past the girl. A girl I want to save, but don't think I can.

My only hope is to convince Felix to free her and then come over to my side.

Felix looks at me, obviously as disturbed as I am about what Milo thinks is acceptable to do to a woman.

"Let's go for our run outside," Felix says.

I raise an eyebrow and try to hide my excitement.

Konrad frowns. "Are you sure that's a good idea?"

"Yes, go grab us some waters," Felix says.

I hesitate a moment, trying to decide what I should do. I want to see outside. I need to see the perimeter and understand Milo's guard rotation and security system better. But I need to save the girl.

Kai would never forgive me if I didn't.

I would never forgive me.

I look down the hallway to where the girl disappeared with one of the guards.

"Are you going to help me save the girl, or am I doing this alone?" I ask.

Felix swallows hard. He's too deep into this world to help me. I don't know what collateral Milo has on him, but he's not going to help me.

"I'll help you, but I won't get caught. And if I do, you owe me a job," Felix says.

I smirk. "Deal."

"Don't think this makes us friends. And don't think I will help you escape."

"I'm not asking you to help me escape. I'm asking you to help me save the girl."

He nods. "What's your plan?"

I grin and crack my neck. It feels good to be doing something useful again.

7

KAI

I sit on the edge of the exam table. The paper gown I'm wearing crinkles as I shift my weight.

The exam was horrible. Not painful exactly, just uncomfortable. I don't know if I'll ever get over other people touching me. I would have much preferred one of the doctors I'm gotten used to that worked for Enzo to examine me, but I needed to go see a specialist. I need answers. As bad as the exam was, the wait for answers is worse.

I shiver as the AC kicks on, making my already cold skin feel like ice. The doctor was shocked when she touched me at how chilly my skin was, but she didn't say anything. Nor did she remark about the scars she saw on my body. She just wanted to know if I was safe.

I chuckle to myself thinking about it. It's such a ridiculous question to someone like me. *Have I ever been safe? Will I ever be safe?*

Enzo has tried ever since he fucked up to keep me protected. Something he might say he's succeeding at, but I know better—he's failing. Because I'm not safe.

The door starts opening. My heart races and the hair on

my arms stand at attention. The doctor always knocks before entering. Whoever is entering isn't the doctor.

I search for a weapon in the room. I didn't bring a gun or a knife with me; I didn't think I would need one at the doctor's office. And I didn't think if they found a gun on me, they'd be too happy. I wanted as few questions as possible.

Fuck, I didn't even bring Langston with me. He's still searching for any long lost family members I might have.

I jump off the table, and all I can find are tongue compressors. I grab them and then exhale sharply.

"You going to try and choke me to death or something?" Liesel says eyeing my pathetic weapons.

"You should have knocked," I say, putting them back on the counter as I pull the paper dress tighter over my body. I reluctantly climb back on the table as Liesel grabs a magazine and takes a seat in one of the chairs in the room.

"What are you doing?" I ask as she flips the page.

"Reading."

I frown. "Liesel?"

She shrugs. "I thought you could use some company while you wait. God knows they've made you wait long enough."

Liesel might be one of the last people on earth I want waiting with me. She's the only other woman Enzo has ever come close to loving. And she loves him as much as I love him. That alone makes us enemies.

"Thanks," I say, swallowing hard as the door finally opens.

Liesel tosses the magazine and sits up.

Dr. Stanton enters, and from the worried look on her face, I know the results aren't good. She ignores Liesel and heads straight for me. The doctor offers to take my hand, but I shake my head. Touching a stranger while getting some of the worst results of my life will destroy me.

But as the doctor starts speaking, I regret the decision. I need touch. I need comfort. I need love. I need something to hold onto. I already knew the truth, but her words will stop all hope.

"I'm sorry, Miss Miller..." she starts.

She might as well have set me on fire, that's how badly her words hurt.

I feel a hand grip mine. I don't look down. I know Liesel is holding my hand, and it doesn't feel like a knife stabbing through my palm. It feels like comfort in one of the most soul-crushing moments of my life.

"...but the results show that you can't have children."

I blink once before the tears start, clouding my vision so I can't see. Not only my present, but my future.

I can't have kids.

I was never sure if I really wanted kids until this moment. Until it was confirmed that I couldn't.

And it hurts. The emptiness is nothing I have ever felt.

I'm alone and have no hope of ever creating a life to continue my own. This life is it. And I'll live it by myself.

I let myself be selfish. I let myself hurt for my own personal reasons. For not being able to have a biological kid. I let the feelings consume me. And only then, when I've cried all the tears for myself, do I cry for what this means for others.

I will never produce an heir. Unless Langston finds a miracle, I have no chance of becoming Black. No chance to use that power to help innocent people. No chance at keeping Milo from winning. And no chance trying to trade myself for Enzo. Milo would never want me now that I have no chance of ever becoming Black.

And I have no idea now how I can save Enzo...

My heart.

My fucking heart.

This pain will never stop. It's suffocating me from the inside out. All the hope I felt after Enzo left and Liesel walked in to pull me from the depths of my desperation is gone. And I'm right back in the moment when Enzo was taken from me.

My body is numb. My cheeks burn with icy tears. My chest barely moves with shallow breaths. And I'm sure my heart has stopped, completely given up on life.

I can't have a kid.

I can't become Black.

I can't save Enzo.

It's too much. All of it.

I need a release, an escape from all it.

I feel a tight squeeze on my hand, and I know the doctor and Liesel are talking. I know they are trying to bring me back from the place I've gone. But they can't. I have to find my way back myself. Enzo is the only one who could ever pull me from the cage I build.

That's what I'm doing—building up walls to block all of this pain out. It's the only way I'll survive.

But I no longer care if I survive.

"NO!" I scream, it's guttural, and deep, and lets out every emotion I'm feeling.

I know I shouldn't yell in a doctor's office, but the shriek was necessary. I'm not thinking. I'm barely existing.

Slowly, I come back down. Liesel is still gripping my hand and gives me a tight smile when I finally look at her. I thought she would give me a smart remark for yelling and crying over not being able to have kids. Many people aren't able to have kids.

But that's not what I see. Liesel's eyes are puffy and red. And there are tears still running down her cheeks.

She looks at me like the news is as much her heartache as it is mine.

When she sees I've finally reentered the real world again, she turns to the doctor. "What options does she have?"

"I'm sorry, but I don't think there is anything I can do," the doctor answers.

"Really? Nothing? You don't have some shots you can give her or surgery or anything to help her?"

She shakes her head softly. "There is just too much damage. I'm sorry."

"What about surrogacy?" Liesel asks, not giving up.

I squeeze her hand, trying to say thanks to her without using my actual words.

The doctor's eyes flutter up to mine, and I know she's going to shatter that dream too. I can have kids. I can adopt. I can find a way to have children if that is what I want, but it won't be enough to help Enzo.

"I'm sorry," the doctor says again. And then I see the tears in the doctor's eyes. "If you need anything else, a support group, information about adoption, anything, please let me know." She squeezes my shoulder, but I don't even register the pain. And then she leaves.

"Fuck her," Liesel says, wiping her eyes.

I turn toward Liesel with wide eyes.

"Fuck her," she says again. "She's a doctor. She's supposed to help people."

"She did her best; it's not her fault that I'm too broken to fix."

Liesel's head snaps. "Oh no, you don't get to go feeling sorry for yourself. Hearing that was heartbreaking. You cried. I cried. The doctor cried. You got to feel the pain, but you don't get to remain broken. Enzo still needs us. The Black company still needs us. Get your shit together."

I frown. *I can't.*

"I can't save Enzo. And the Black empire deserves a strong leader."

"Get the fuck up," Liesel says, done with my moping. Apparently, the five minutes I allowed myself to cry is all I'm allowed.

"Up!" Liesel tugs on my arm, and I stand up.

She heads to the door.

"I'm still wearing the paper gown."

Liesel rolls her eyes and throws clothes at me. "Then get dressed if you don't want to flash everyone."

I hurriedly change back into my jeans and T-shirt. And then I follow Liesel out of the office.

We hop into her Maserati, and I stare out the window, reminding my heart to beat and my lungs to breathe every other second so I stay alive. Right now, staying alive is the best I can hope for.

———

I don't realize where we are going until we are stopped outside the club.

"What are we doing at Surrender?" I ask.

"Reminding you that there is more at stake than just you and Enzo."

Liesel hops out and flicks her keys to one of the valets. I slowly climb out afterward.

I don't want to go in the place filled with Enzo's belongings. I don't want to face all the men I'm not worthy of leading.

But Liesel won't give me a choice. At least I can drink away my sorrows here.

I step inside and watch as Liesel struts. She's wearing leather pants that hug her hips and a light grey sleeveless shirt that shows off her toned arms and just the right amount of cleavage.

She tosses her hair back, and every man in the room watches her do it.

I've never been envious of another woman before, but Liesel makes me jealous in a way I didn't think was possible.

She scours the room as if looking for her prey. And in a second, she focuses in on her target.

I follow her eyes and find Langston sitting with a drink in his hand and the attention of every woman in the bar. Langston has a reputation for being a bit of a manwhore, but I haven't seen it much myself. Mostly because I was always too focused on Enzo. Or I was hanging out with Zeke.

But watching him now, every woman is flocking to him. He's not attractive in the same way that Enzo is, or even Zeke was. Enzo is dark, controlling, and power. Zeke was all muscle and strength, his muscles pouring out of him hiding everything else. But Langston is more clean cut. His hair is short and perfectly styled. His clothes fit his toned but not bulky muscles. He has a few tattoos, but not enough to make him look like a bad boy. His blue eyes are what draw in the women, and his sultry smile is what seals the deal.

His dimply smile disappears when he spots Liesel—glaring at him like he fucked up in the worst possible way. And I can't help myself.

"Is there something going on between you two?"

"No, and there never will be. He's a manwhore. He can't

even keep it in his pants when he's supposed to be working."

Liesel stomps off toward the offices.

I follow and collapse into the chair Enzo usually sits in. I take a deep breath, savoring his musky scent.

Liesel paces, waiting for Langston to enter.

"A peace offering," Langston says, holding up two margaritas. He hands one to me and the other to Liesel.

"You are supposed to be working to find a relative of Kai's, not flirting and fucking every woman within a five-mile radius," Liesel snaps.

"Actually, my radius is ten. Women have no problem traveling to ride my cock," Langston says.

I ignore both of them. "Did you find anything, Langston?"

He winces. "You seem to be the last Miller left. Other than your father, I couldn't find anyone."

I close my eyes, trying not to let the news affect me. I knew this was probably going to happen anyway.

"What about you? How did your appointment go?" Langston asks.

"Really, Langston? Read the room," Liesel says sharply.

Langston collapses into the chair next to me, obviously reading between the lines.

"I'm sorry," he says. When the doctor said she was sorry, it felt a little empty and cold. But when Langston says it, every syllable of his apology is dripping with the same pain I feel.

We are all silent for a moment. I work on gulping down my margarita. The empty sound the straw makes as I suck up the last of the liquid brings us all back.

They smile lightly at my slurping.

"So, what happens now?" Langston asks.

"I'm not sure. I guess I keep competing while we try to find any other way to find me a successor that fits the rules to keep Milo from taking the empire. And we try to find a way to save Enzo," I say.

But I have no idea how to do any of those things.

The silence starts again, because none of us have answers. And honestly, I've given up hope of keeping Milo from taking the empire. All I can think about is finding a way to save Enzo.

A knock on the door brings us back to life. A man pokes his head in.

"Um..." he says, looking around the room. "Who is in charge? Is Enzo here?"

"No, I'm in charge while he's gone," I say.

He nods and enters. "A new client is here. She says she needs a security system and protection. I don't know who she's running from, but it's bad. She's scared shitless. I told her I would have one of you go talk to her and decide if we can take her on as a client, but from the look of her, I doubt she has much money."

"Bring her to Langston's office, and tell her I'll be right there," I say.

This is bigger than just saving Enzo. Although, I wish that was all this was because saving Enzo would be easy. Gather all our men and attack, get Enzo out, and put him into hiding. But the Black empire is so much more. It has the ability to help so many people.

And if Milo gets his hands on it, then women like this will have nowhere to turn—that can't happen.

I stand up. "I'm going to go help this woman, which is what this organization should be using its power—helping those that need protection. And if Enzo or I get to have full control, that is how we will use that power. We can't let Milo win.

"When I get back, I want every idea you two have on how to stop Milo from becoming Black. Either find me an heir or convince Enzo to change his heir from Milo to his own child or a different relative."

"What about saving Enzo?" Liesel asks.

"I already know how to save Enzo."

"How?" Liesel asks, staring into my soul. And I know she can read me as well as Enzo can. Maybe I wear my feelings on my sleeve too clearly.

"You already know the answer to that. It's the only solution I've ever had."

She nods.

And Enzo is going to hate me for it, but it might be the best way to save the empire as well.

8

ENZO

THE BEDROOM IS dark when I enter. Felix got me in, but that was all he could do. He can't risk his life to help me save the girl. And if Milo finds out he helped me, he will kill him, so I'll have to tell Milo I escaped on my own if he finds out what I've done.

But for now, I have more important things to focus on, like finding a way to actually save the girl, so this won't all be for nothing.

The lights are off, but it's not pitch dark like the dungeon Milo keeps me in. This bedroom screams luxury. The bed is an oversized king with gold and white sheets and a canopy overhead that looks like the bed belongs in heaven instead of this hell of a house. The floor is slick hardwood, and there are large mirrors on every wall, including the ceiling.

So the bastard can watch himself as he rapes women —disgusting.

But what I don't see is the girl the guard brought here. *Did we get the wrong room?*

"Don't take another step," the girl's shaky voice orders.

I stop. I don't want to scare her, but I don't have a lot of time to convince her to trust me.

"It's okay, I won't hurt you," I say, trying to make my voice sound sweet. But it still comes out deeper and darker than I intended.

I spot the girl in the corner of the room. Her body trembles, and she's holding a lamp in her hand.

I smile. She found a weapon, but that's not enough to protect her. I'm her only hope.

The fear is palpable in the room. It oozes from her body and fills the air. A man like Milo gets off on it, but me it pisses off and takes me to a dark place. A place where Kai was hurt, beaten, and tortured. A place she endured for six years because I was too stupid to go and save her.

I could save a thousand women like the one standing in front of me, and it still wouldn't be enough to absolve me of my sins.

"Let me help you," I say, not bothering to extend my hand. Even if this woman hasn't already been beaten like Kai, I'm sure she still won't want to be touched. Kai taught me a lot about what is needed to get permission to touch a woman—trust. And I haven't earned this woman's trust yet. Even if I save her from Milo, it probably won't be enough.

"Leave me alone," she hisses.

"I can't."

She trembles. She doesn't see me as her ally. She sees me as her enemy.

I'm desperate to take a step toward her. I want to quickly scoop her up and drag her out of here. But she'll yell and scream and draw more attention. And I don't want to traumatize her if I don't have to.

"I'm a prisoner too. I was the man in the hallway. The

man with the bruises and crooked nose. The man with the two guards watching me."

I hold out my hands, trying to show her the permanent scars on my wrists from the rope Milo used. But it's dark, and we are twenty feet away, I doubt she can see the marks.

"Just leave," she says sadly.

"I can't. I need to help you escape. I can't let you get hurt. I made a promise to a woman to save her, and by extension, any innocent woman like her. I won't let Milo hurt you, which is what will happen if you stay. He will rape you. He might even try to get you pregnant because he needs an heir. But either way, the end will be the same. He will kill you."

She gasps.

Fuck, maybe I messed up. I shouldn't have been so crass and honest with her.

"Trust me. I may not be an angel, but I'm in the business of saving angels."

I hold out my hand, hoping she will come to me. Because I really don't want to frighten her.

Her arms tremble from holding the heavy lamp up. She finally sets it down on the floor.

Progress.

I hear a noise in the hallway, and I know we don't have much time.

"I need you to take my hand or tell me that you can't. And if you can't, I will save you anyway," I say.

I watch her chest rise and fall. She has brown, almost black hair like Kai, but not quite as dark. Her body is thin, but her eyes look brown, unlike the piercing green-blue of Kai's.

This woman has only been here a few minutes, and Milo has already taken her strength and fire. She will live the rest of her life scared, looking over her shoulder, assuming every man is bad. Milo already took so much from her; he doesn't get to take any more.

"What is your name?" I try.

"Ariel."

"Ariel, I need you to trust me. Can you take my hand?"

She shakes her head.

Fuck!

Her body shakes along with her head. I really don't want to hurt her.

"Can I pick you up and take you somewhere safe?"

She stops moving.

The weight of the air is heavy, and I feel it on my chest. I need to save her so badly. I need to do something useful to make up for the pain I caused Kai.

And then I see the spark of hope I need—her tiny head nods. Just once, but I know it was real.

I approach her slowly, and she doesn't retreat.

"I'm going to lift you now. Close your eyes. And open them when I say you are safe," I coddle.

She closes her eyes, and I lift her tiny body into my arms. That was the easy part. Now I have to find a way out of here where she will be safe.

I carry her to the door, and poke my head out. Felix spots me.

"One of the maids left her keys in the car around back. The Fiat. Get her to the car. She'll be able to drive out of here without being stopped," Felix says.

I glance down at the limp body in my arms, barely hanging on and all she has to do right now is keep breathing.

"And what if she can't drive herself?" I ask.

He runs his hand through his hair. "Jesus. I'll drive her. But if I do, I can't come back."

Fuck, I need Felix here. I need a friend—but that's selfish of me.

"Let's go," I say, hoping I can figure out a way to get her out of here while keeping Felix here.

We already disconnected the security system, so there are no cameras on us. But there are still guards.

Felix leads us to the car without any issue. We don't meet any guards. And the woman in my arms keeps her eyes closed, shutting herself down to prevent any pain that could come her way.

I place her in the back of the small Fiat hatchback, lying her in the floor so she can't be seen through the windows.

"You are going to have to drive her," I say.

But then the door locks beep.

We both crouch down behind the car.

Footsteps approach but they are soft and light on gravel.

"Have a great holiday," a woman shouts.

"I will! See you next week," the woman approaching the car says.

"Can we trust her not to turn the girl in once she discovers she's in the back seat of her car?" I ask Felix.

He nods. "If for no other reason than she would fear Milo would think she was one that helped her. I would guess she won't come back to work next week; she'll be too afraid."

I hate that I'm ending the maid's income here and that she will need to find a new job, but she shouldn't be working for a man like Milo. Nothing is stopping him from doing the same thing to her as he was planning to do to the girl in her backseat.

So we slink back into the bushes as the maid drives

away with her stowaway. We watch silently as she makes it through the gate, and then we both re-enter the house.

Felix takes me back to my cell, hoping Milo will think the girl got away on her own.

I don't have the same hope that Felix has. I want Milo to find out. It will give me another excuse to fight him.

Within the hour, I hear the familiar sound of Milo stomping down the stairs. I look up from the book I had been flipping through to try and distract me while I waited.

He gets to the bars and stares at me with all of his furry.

"What did you do?" he asks.

I toss my book on the bed.

"I don't know what you mean. I've been working out and reading—my usual routine."

He studies me a moment, and I think maybe I've gotten away with it. But then he determines my guilt and carries out my sentence a second later by putting a bullet into my shoulder.

I grit my teeth to keep from screaming at the sudden unexpected impact and collapse on my mattress. People say getting shot doesn't hurt because it happens so fast; that it's only the pain after the adrenaline has worn off that hurts. Those people are liars. Getting shot hurts. Not being able to fight back hurts worse.

Slowly, I pull myself off the bed and walk to the bars to face him.

"So that's how it's going to be. Just shoot me without giving me a chance to fight back."

"You set my whore free without giving me a chance to stop it."

"You don't get to hurt women like that."

The change in Milo's eyes is fast and sharp. I've only

ever seen the look in my father's eyes when he felt I wasn't strong enough.

How do Milo and my father share the same eyes?

"I need an heir. I need to fuck a woman and get her pregnant. But since you took away my best option, I think I know the perfect candidate for the job," Milo says.

"You can't touch Kai," I say, throwing my body against the bars to try and reach Milo. But he calmly takes a step backward.

"I think I will. She has strong hips. I'm sure they are big enough to bear my children."

"Don't. Touch. Her."

Another shot. This time I only register the sound of the gun going off, not the sting in my other shoulder. I don't feel the blood pooling or the throb of my muscles, because all I feel is anger toward Milo. And fear that he might actually take Kai.

He grins. "How do you know I haven't already?"

He's lying. He doesn't have Kai. I can see behind his cocky grin. He wants to hurt me as I hurt him. He needs to get back at me for taking his woman.

"What do you want, Milo? I'll give it to you," I say.

"Nothing you can give. I'll be taking Kai when I'm good and ready."

"And if you do, I'll change the documents so your child is no longer my heir. You will never become Black if you take her. She can't make you her heir."

Our eyes lock in an endless battle. I've never hated a man as much as I hate Milo. I hated my father. Hated him for what he made me do, but it was nothing compared to Milo. Although, I guess my father never lived long enough to threaten Kai's life. But he would have. He ordered me to kill Kai. He would have made me follow through on that threat if he had lived.

I sent my father to hell. And I plan on doing the same to Milo as soon as it is safe to.

"Yes?" Milo snaps into the phone he decides to answer.

But then he turns his back to me as he listens carefully to the conversation. His shoulders tense, his legs stop moving, and his face grows white.

He ends the call and then turns back to me. And I know exactly who it was.

"Archard called?" I ask.

Milo's eyes are wide, his lips tense, and his jaw set. He nods slowly.

"When is the next game?"

"Tomorrow."

He looks like I just told him he only has a few hours left to live.

And then I remember, he just shot me in both of my shoulders. I need to be recovering, not fighting in whatever game tomorrow. I'm going to have to spend the next several hours on a plane flying back to Miami. I'm going to be in no shape to fight and win. And it's all Milo's fault.

His face is fear, matching my own. I should be happy he just ruined his chance of winning this game, but I'm not. Milo is unpredictable. There is no telling what he will do if I lose.

And I can't risk losing Kai.

Tomorrow I will get to see her again. Tomorrow I will have to face the heartbreak. Tomorrow I will have to convince Milo he needs me and not her. Tomorrow...

9

KAI

Enzo Black has saved so many women.

Hundreds.

All in desperate need of saving and no one to turn to but him.

Most he's saved since taking over the title of Black from his father, but even before his father died, Enzo was still saving women in secret.

This was Enzo's burden. He didn't talk to anyone else about it. And unless he couldn't handle it himself, he didn't even get his crew involved. But every single woman that came to him for help, he saved.

A tear rolls down my cheek as my heart hurts for Enzo. For the boy who lost his mother way too young—he couldn't save her.

For his childhood friend who was hurt way too young—he couldn't save Liesel.

Even the love of his life was taken—he couldn't save me.

Enzo couldn't save any of the women he cared for and loved. But he could save all of the strangers who came to him in the dark.

I flip through file after file of women he helped. Women who were running from abusers. Women who were taken and needed to be found. Women who were killed and needed avenging. Women who were broken and needed healing.

He saved them all.

He rescued them with weapons. Healed them by finding their families or paying for therapy. And sparked a new life in them by helping them find a job or career that could support them, even though none of the women needed the money. Enzo found every man who ever hurt them, and made them pay the women millions for the pain they caused them.

I wipe the tear from my cheek. *How could Enzo think he wasn't anything but an angel?*

His father may have tried to turn him into a cruel bastard, but the good in Enzo resisted. Even as a child. And even now. Even when I pulled out the darkest part of him, he only fucked up for a moment before realizing his mistake.

Enzo is human, but to so many women, he's so much more. He's their knight coming to rescue them when they have given up hope of anyone finding them.

I lean back in my chair, trying to make sense of what needs to happen. I can't be Black. But Enzo deserves to be.

He has everything needed to be Black.

Strength.

Courage.

And heart.

If truly given all the power and resources, Enzo could turn the hundreds of women he's saved into thousands.

A rattle on the door stops my train of thought.

I look up and see Langston standing in my doorway.

I smile lightly and wipe the rest of my tears from my eyes as she steps into the office.

He looks down at the files of women scattered all over the desk.

"Did you know about this?" I ask.

He nods. "Only Zeke and I knew." Langston chuckles, shaking his head. "Enzo never wanted the world to see the goodness in him; he thought it was weakness. I guess you can thank his father for that twisted thinking."

I brush my hand over the last file.

"We have to help him. Enzo deserves to be Black. The world needs him."

Langston nods. "The world would be better off with Enzo as Black over Milo."

"Then you will help me? You will help me make the trade?" I ask, meaning my life for Enzo's.

Langston rubs his neck as he paces in the small office. His eyes drift up as he studies a picture on the wall. Some sort of black and white abstract painting.

Finally, Langston turns back to me, "I want to, Kai. I really want to. I need Enzo back as much as you do. I already lost Zeke; he made up one-third of who I am. Enzo made up the other third. I'm not whole without the two of them. I can't bring Zeke back, but I can Enzo."

"Then help me."

His eyes tighten, and he bites his lip. "I can't, stingray."

I frown. "Why not?"

"Because Zeke would never forgive me."

I huff. "Zeke wouldn't forgive you? Are you serious? Zeke would totally forgive you for saving Enzo."

Langston walks over to me and kneels in front of me on one leg. He looks so serious kneeling there.

"Are you about to propose? Because I can save you some

trouble-the only man I would ever marry is Enzo," I tease, stroking his cheek. It's rough from his stubble.

He takes my hand, and I really don't know what he's doing.

"I want to save Enzo, but not by losing you. I won't trade you for him. Zeke wouldn't forgive me. Enzo wouldn't forgive me. I wouldn't forgive me."

He kisses the back of my hand. "Zeke protected you, and it cost him his life. Enzo saved you, and it cost him his empire and possibly his life. I'm not going to let their sacrifices be for nothing. Which is what would happen if you save Enzo."

I frown. I can't fight Milo, Enzo, and Langston at the same time. I need Langston on my side.

"What if I don't have to sacrifice myself to save Enzo?"

He smiles sadly. "You know that's the only way, and I'm not going to let that happen. I'd die before I let Milo or any man take you."

"I can't let Enzo sacrifice for me. Zeke shouldn't have. And I'm not going to let you die for me either."

"Is Enzo worthy of saving? Does the good he's done absolve his sins?"

"Yes."

"That's how we all feel about you, but even more so because your crimes are nothing compared to Enzo's. And the good you could do, if given the chance, would triumph over anything Enzo is capable of."

"But I haven't done any good."

"Oh, stingray, you have no idea what you have done. You healed a man so broken we all thought he couldn't be saved. You made him love. And you gained the love and trust of Zeke and me, two men who have given up that idea completely. You showed us what true strength is. You should be Black. *You.*"

"But I can't—"

His thumb brushes against my bottom lip, shutting me up. He looks up with his dreamy eyes. He really is an attractive man. And if I wasn't so hung up on Enzo, I would give a man like Langston a chance. But I'm hopelessly Enzo's, and Langston is nothing more than an overprotective brother to me.

And despite his touch, I know he feels the same.

"Let me worry about the rules. I'll find you an heir. I don't know how yet. But I'll find some way. Some loophole in the rules. Or some person whose DNA matches yours. Or some technology that can help you have a child. This is how I will save you. Zeke and Enzo played their roles in your rise to power, let me find a way to help you."

I swallow the lump in my throat. Three men. Three wonderful, powerful men. All willing to lay their lives down for me. All thinking I'm more worthy than them.

What if I fail them?

What if I do become Black?

What if I'm not good enough?

What if their sacrifices were for nothing?

Langston exhales with a smile. "Stop worrying if you are worthy. The fact that you worry about being enough is what makes you the most worthy of us all."

I nod, unable to speak words. I know Langston will keep his promise, which means I have a chance at becoming Black. *But at what cost? I can't be Black if it means losing Enzo forever.*

"Miss Miller," Archard says at the door, not bothering to knock.

Langston stands but keeps his hand on my shoulder as

if he's become my shield protecting me from whatever words Archard has come here to speak.

"Tomorrow is game day," Archard says.

Tomorrow. I get to see Enzo tomorrow. And it will most likely demolish what is left of my heart.

I only have until tomorrow to figure out if I can save Enzo. And from the grip of the man standing next to me, I know it's not possible. Langston won't let me save Enzo, not this time. I will have to wait until the last game. By then, Enzo will know everything there is to know about Milo. By then, we will know exactly who our enemy is and how strong he is. By then, one of us will become Black, and we will have no choice but to fight against Milo, no matter the personal cost.

I have to wait, until the last game. *But what if I can't wait?*

10

ENZO

I FEEL HIGH—THAT'S how many painkillers I'm on.

The doctors tug on my skin, but I don't feel it. They've been working on my shoulders the entire flight to Miami. Removing bullet fragments, preventing infection, closing the wound, doing therapy on my shoulders to ensure I still have full range of motion, filling my body with more blood and painkillers to the point that I don't feel any pain. I wouldn't be surprised if Milo had them pump some performance-enhancing drug into my system to try and ensure I win.

This isn't like any other sporting competition. There will be no testing for drugs. No calls that I competed unfairly.

And still, after all the work and drugs, I know I won't win. Even if I was healthy, this game was designed by Kai's father. He designed it for her to win. I'll win the fourth game, which means it will come down to the fifth game. The one where neither of us will have an advantage because our fathers had to create it together.

"You look like crap," Milo says, staring at me on the makeshift hospital table as we land in Miami.

"Then maybe you shouldn't have shot me if you cared how I looked."

"Let's go, we don't want to be late."

I throw on a black T-shirt to cover my wounds, and I don't even feel the fabric brush my skin. I feel too good. I feel invincible. And all I want to do is attack Milo.

We exit the plane and load into the back of one of the blacked out SUV's, and then we head toward Surrender.

Milo sits in the front of the car looking anxious. I don't know why he needs me to win so badly. Why does he want my empire? It goes deeper than just our last interactions. This goes years deeper.

It's the one question I still don't have an answer to. My time with him has taught me everything else. The guards to trust, and those who are loyal to Milo. The layout of his mansion and the secret passageways underneath. The security system he uses and how many guards are hidden outside. I know everything. Everything except why he holds a grudge against me. Everything except how many enemies of mine he has ready to fight if he asks. I know everything but the most important things.

We arrive at Surrender, and to my surprise, Milo doesn't have me tied up. Maybe he thinks it would cause more damage to my shoulders if he did. Instead, he has his men surround me, guarding me as we walk into my club.

As soon as we enter, the room falls silent. All of the men stare at us, and glare at Milo. Some men salute me or lower their hats in respect for me. One man even bows as if I'm a king. It melts my insides to know that despite everything, my men still believe I'm their leader. *What would happen if Milo were to become Black? How many would follow him? How many would revolt and die fighting him?*

If Milo wins, I need to find a way to keep the employees safe—I owe them that.

We walk to my office and step inside. At first, I can't see who is in the room. The men surrounding me block my view with their bodies. But then, Kai comes into view.

Her hair is braided down her back, she's not wearing any makeup, and wears a curve-hugging black shirt and leather pants I'm pretty sure belong to Liesel. She looks fierce and unstoppable.

She keeps her face stoic and unchanging when I walk into the room. As if her heart isn't breaking all over again. But I can hear the change in her heartbeat. I can feel the change from warm to cool in the air. I can see the change in her breathing from slow to rapid.

We are the only two people who exist in this moment even though the room is crowded. And I can see the moment she realizes I'm hurt. She can sense me as easily as I can feel her.

Her pupils dilate in anger for a split second, but I'm the only one who notices. She stares at my shoulders as if she can see through my shirt to the pain masked by the drugs.

She grits her teeth to keep from growling. And I know she wants to run and attack Milo for what he did to me.

She glances his way for a second, as she lets her shield down to me. And I finally feel all of her pain. She hurts for me, but she mourns her own loss too. The loss of carrying a child. She confirmed her truth. She can't have a baby. And she hasn't found a blood relative she can make her heir.

Her hope is lost.

And it makes me crazy.

Finally, the connection we share is severed as I notice the other two people standing next to her—Langston and

Liesel. Both are dressed just as fiercely as Kai, as if they are ready to do battle alongside her.

I smile, thinking back to the first game, where everyone was on my side, and no one was on Kai's. I prefer it this way, even if it would make it easier if she just bowed down and let me win. She can't become Black, even if she wins every game left. The rules demand an heir. And she can't produce one.

Just let me win so we can end this as quickly as possible.

All of their eyes focus on Milo, giving him various shades of glaring, growling, and snickering.

"Does he really need to be here?" Liesel points to Milo as she talks to Archard.

"Each competitor is allowed to bring whoever they want to watch the competition," Archard says.

Liesel crosses her arms as she stares at Milo. "No one wants you here."

Milo leans into her, "Your nipples disagree."

Liesel's nipples are pointed, but it's just because the room is so cold from Kai being in it. I know Kai doesn't have any magical powers, but somehow she always brings the cold chill she always carries with her wherever she goes.

Liesel won't let a comment like that go, "It would be the last thing your cock ever did."

Milo jolts forward as if he's going to hit her for her comment, but Liesel stands her ground and just raises her eyebrow. Langston jumps forward, ready to fight Milo.

Archard clears his throat, dissipating the almost fight.

"If you are all ready, I'd like to read the rules of the next game," he says.

Everyone quiets and faces him.

"This is the third game. Currently, you are both tied one

to one. As this is the third game, Mr. Miller, Kai's father, was the one who set the rules."

We all nod as he drags out what the game is.

"Mr. Miller believed that the person who becomes Black needed to have the strength to face any amount of pain and do it with compassion, humility, and beauty. You need to be able to withstand torture without breaking. Pain without losing yourself. But above all, do the right thing."

I can't look at Kai as Archard speaks, because this is already sounding like this game is going to be my own personal hell.

"What are the rules, old man? How many rounds of torture does each have to endure to win? Does one of them have to surrender for the other to win? Because we already know who will be surrendering," Milo says giving Kai a dirty look.

Archard glares at Milo, not willing to take his crap. "Only the two competitors are allowed to ask questions. If you speak again, you will be removed."

Milo huffs but shuts up.

"As I was saying, this game is about withstanding torture and pain with grace. I will not share how many rounds of torture there are or what each round will include, but each round will become more painful and difficult to bear. The game ends when one of you surrenders."

Fuck, Mr. Miller, he's more twisted than my own father. That's why he had Kai kidnapped, so she was prepared to deal with pain. So she could win this round. She learned to lock away her pain. She can withstand any torture.

My father taught me to handle pain as well, but Kai is better at it. And I will have to watch her being tortured. It will kill me. The torture won't be physical for me. The drugs will mask any pain I feel. I'm usually good at handling pain, but this will make it even harder. My weakness is Kai. If she shows any amount of pain, I will lose it.

"Each of you must choose a teammate who will carry out the torture of the other competitor," Archard says.

Kai's eyes meet Langston's. She would never ask Liesel to do it, even though it might hurt me more to have Liesel torturing me. Langston nods.

"Langston," Kai says, sucking in a breath.

"Good," Archard says, turning to me.

I close my eyes because I already know who my only choice is, and I can't do it. I can't make her suffer that way, even if it might be my only chance of winning.

Milo clears his throat, and then he whispers in my ear. "If you don't win, I will hurt Kai."

He won't. Langston and I won't let him, but it's enough to push me into saying my choice. "Milo, I choose Milo."

Kai's eyes burn into mine. Milo is going to be the one to end this game early. And I don't know if Milo is going to break Kai or me. Because the pain will intensify as Milo is the one who is carrying out the torture, but the pain at watching him touch her will explode my own suffering.

Either way, I'm screwed.

11

KAI

THE SECOND I saw Enzo I could fully breathe again. The kind of breath that fills your lungs and energizes your body with new hope.

But then I saw the damage. I felt the extra heat pulsing through his body before I figured out where the pain was coming from.

And I wanted to kill Milo, more than I did before. I wanted to destroy him. Make him pay with his life for laying a finger on my man.

Enzo was supposed to be safe. Milo needed him to take over the Black empire, but apparently, he didn't care to not hurt him in the process.

Both of Enzo's shoulders are damaged. And I want to run over to him, put my arms around his, and drag his ass as far away from these people as possible.

Instead, I'm about to play the most twisted game of all.

Thank you, father.

I exhale deeply. *I can do this.*

But I can't. I can't watch Enzo being tortured knowing he's already in pain. The game isn't how much can I withstand torture, because I can indefinitely, it's how much can I watch the man I love being beaten.

"Torture is killing each other slowly, death by a thousand cuts," Archard reads from a paper in front of him. "So before each round the tormenter will get to stab once into their victim at the place of their choosing." Archard produces one small knife and hands it to Milo.

"Each round will alternate who goes first. Kai is first this round," Archard continues.

I feel Milo walking over to me with his knife in hand as Langston walks toward Enzo. Liesel is still standing on my left side, and I hear her tiny gasp as Milo pushes the blade into my shoulder without any warning.

I don't flinch. Instead, my eyes bare into Enzo's. There were hundreds of more painful places Milo could have stabbed me, but he chose the place Enzo was already hurt so I could remember what he did to Enzo and what pain he is in.

My eyes flicker to Langston, and I beg him to go easy on Enzo. I need him to go easy if I want a chance at winning.

Langston presses his knife into Enzo's thigh through his jeans, and when he pulls the knife, I see how little damage he has done and exhale.

Jesus, I'm not going to survive this.

It was just a tiny nick, Enzo didn't flinch. He didn't feel it any more than I did.

I feel sick to my stomach though. And I hate my father even more than I ever thought possible.

Milo snickers behind my shoulder. He's going to use my hatred for Milo against me. I can't let him win.

"Now that we got the formalities out of the way, it's time for the first round. Remember each round will get more difficult and that at any time if you would like to stop, just say so, and the game is over," Archard says.

I nod. Enzo just stares at Archard.

"The first round will test your ability to be alone without food or water. You will each be hidden in a room of your tormentor's choosing. I will not tell you how long you will be in the room, but it will be long enough to test both of your willpowers," Archard says. He looks to Milo. "Milo please take your prisoner to a dark room of your choosing. It must be in Miami, otherwise, there are no rules. Once you have selected your place, then Langston can choose his place."

Milo grins and grabs my wrist forcibly. "My pleasure."

Damn, why does his touch burn so much? Am I ever going to get over the feeling of a single touch like this?

But what hurts worse is being pulled away from Enzo. This first round will be nothing for either of us. It will barely cause either of us pain. We are used to being alone, and going without food or water is as easy as breathing for us. But my solace, and my punishment, was that we would complete each round in front of each other. This is the easiest round, and instead of getting to enjoy our time together, breathing the same air, and sending silent messages to each other, we will spend it apart.

"Come on whore," Milo says, tightening his grip. I don't notice if men are following us, and I have no idea where Milo will take me. But I find myself tripping over my feet as we stumble downstairs.

My eyes widen at the small roomed cells beneath the building. "How did you know this was here?"

"Because every bad man has a cell where he keeps the enemies he has to torture."

He tosses me inside roughly, and I fall to the dirt floor. I watch his eyes turn a dark red before he slams the door on my face.

Milo is going to enjoy every second of this game too much. There is something seriously wrong with him.

I stand up and dust myself off, taking in my surroundings. There isn't much in the room Milo has chosen for me. The room is made of thick wooden walls. The floor is dirt, and that ends my tour of the room. There is no furniture, no comforting items, nothing.

I sit down and lean against one of the wooden walls. When I rest my hand against the dirt, I find a rock—entertainment.

I smile as I toss the rock in the air, seeing how high I can toss it and still catch it. I try to focus on the rock instead of missing Enzo. That's how I'll pass the first hours. And then when that gets tiring, I'll sleep. I'm a master at sleeping on a hard floor with an ache in my belly. That's what I did every day for six years. I know this round won't last anywhere near that long.

A door creaks outside, and my ears perk up, listening carefully to the sound.

"You can't lock him in there," Milo says.

"I can too. You chose your prison cell; now, I get to choose mine. And I choose this one," Langston says.

"Then I would like to change the cell for Kai," Milo says.

"You have already selected, Milo. Now Langston gets to select. You can't change your spot. Now I suggest everyone go home and get some sleep; this is going to be a long game," Archard says.

I hear a door lock shut and then footsteps retreating.

Could it be?

As soon as the footsteps stop making their way up the stairs, I run to the wall next to mine. "Enzo?" I ask, cautiously hopeful. I try to keep my heart from speeding up at the thought of spending the night next to Enzo. Being able to hear his voice would be a gift, even though I can't see or touch him.

"You hanging in there, stingray?" Enzo says back.

I sigh into the wall as my heart beats to incredible speeds.

"Your heart is beating so fast," he says against the wall.

"Because of you."

"I know. Mine is just as fast."

I smile. "I can't do this. I can't watch you get hurt—"

"Shh, let's not talk about the game. Let's just enjoy the time we have together."

"How do your shoulders feel?" I ask.

"Milo had me stitched up by the best doctors. I don't think I'll drop dead from an infection or anything," Enzo tries to tease, but I can't joke at a time like this.

My tongue wags around in my mouth as I contemplate what I'm going to say next. "How has he treated you, other than your shoulders?"

"In a cell better than this. He lets me out to exercise and feeds me well. I'd say he treats me as well as any owner would treat their prized racehorse."

"What did you do to make him change and hurt you?"

A pause. "It doesn't matter. How has Langston been treating you?"

"Like a princess. Although, do him and Liesel have a thing for each other?"

Enzo chuckles. "Those two have too much sexual tension between them. But I always thought their hate for each other is what made them keep their hands to themselves. That and Liesel was always too hung up on me to act on any feelings toward any other man."

"They haven't acted on their feelings, and I think that is the problem. They haven't stopped fighting."

"About what?"

I pause considering but answer honestly. "About you."

The silence hangs in the air.

"Are you not going to talk to me now?" I ask.

"Langston wasn't supposed to try and save me. He was supposed to keep you safe—he promised."

"And he kept that promise to keep me safe. He won't risk letting me get hurt to save you. He just wanted to consider if there was any way to save you while keeping me safe. Don't worry, you martyr, he found no option."

I can hear Enzo exhale on the other side of the door and realize telling each other what has happened lately isn't helping.

"Play truth or lies with me," I say.

"Why? So you can try to extract more information out of me?"

"No, so we can enjoy what little time we have left together. I don't want to play anything serious. Just ridiculous facts that neither of us know about each other."

"Fine," he says like he's sulking, but I can feel his smile from here.

"I'll start. Truth or lie? I have a tattoo."

He laughs. "Lie. You forget, I have seen and explored your naked body many times. But I definitely like this game, if it's going to let me think about your naked body more."

I laugh. "Actually...it's the truth."

"What? I don't believe you. I've never seen a tattoo."

"It's on the back of my neck, but it's so small I doubt you would have seen it."

"What is it of?" I ask.

"It was supposed to be of a wave, but all the tattoo artist

got was a thin line before I couldn't take the pain anymore and jumped out of his chair."

"You couldn't handle the pain? Really? You expect me to believe that?"

"I was fourteen and didn't like needles."

This cracks him up. His laughs carry throughout the entire dungeon. "Well, hopefully, your father didn't include an activity involving needles."

I laugh, even though now the thought of getting a tattoo doesn't even register on my pain scale. Maybe someday, I'll go back and finish that tattoo. "Your turn."

His chuckles slowly drift away, and I realize how much I wish our life was so different. I wish we could just live on his yacht, and I could come up with funny stories to make him laugh.

"Truth or lie: I've never had ice cream," he says.

"You've never had ice cream?!"

He chuckles. "Truth or lie?"

"That has to be a lie."

"Truth—my father didn't believe in letting me enjoy any pleasures in life that weren't good for me. And I never thought to try the stuff as an adult."

"When this is all over, we are getting you some freaking ice cream."

I can feel his grin reach his eyes at that. He doesn't say there is a good chance we will never get out of here together. And that makes me happy. Maybe he has more hope than I thought.

"Your turn," he says.

"I punched a boy when I was five."

"Truth."

"Yep, Mason, my only friend. He tried to kiss me, and I punched him."

"That's my girl."

I smile.

"But I win. I punched a boy when I was three?" he asks.

"Truth. I can just see toddler you going around and punching people." I pause. "I've never paid for a drink."

"Truth, you always stole your drinks."

"Or had unsuspecting men pay for them."

We continue on back and forth, saying things we've never done or experienced that should have been part of a normal childhood. We laugh and forget about what the next round is most likely going to bring. We don't formulate a plan of how we are going to beat the game. Or how we are going to take down Milo. We don't discuss if Enzo has a better plan other than turning over everything to him.

But after a few hours, I can tell Enzo is done with the games.

"What are you thinking?" I ask.

"How badly I want to fuck you."

My smile drops. It's the one thing I want more than anything, but there is a thick wall separating us. There is no way to touch each other.

"Me too."

"Ever had phone sex, beautiful?"

I blush. "No."

"Well, that's what we are doing then. Pretend you are on the phone with me, and we are going to have phone sex."

"I don't know how to have phone sex."

"Easy. You just say dirty things you want to do to me, and then I do them to myself. And I'll do the same for you."

"Okay," I breathe, liking the idea too much. I can already feel myself dripping with the thought of hearing dirty words whispered through a tattered wall.

"Sit down on the floor and spread your legs," Enzo says.

I lean against the wall, and do as he says. I put my feet flat on the floor and my knees in the air as I let my thighs open.

"You do the same with your back against the wall," I say.

I close my eyes as I feel Enzo's presence against our common wall.

"Now picture me in your head. I'm kissing your lips, and my tongue slips into your open, wet mouth," Enzo says.

I part my lips and touch my finger to them, imagining Enzo's lips are kissing me. Before this game is all over, I need a real kiss. And the second our lips touch I'm never letting them go again.

"How does it feel?" Enzo asks.

"Your lips feel incredible, but I want more. I want your tongue caressing mine, claiming all of me."

"It is, my tongue is devouring yours. And it's causing you to make that throaty moan you do when you get swept away by my kisses."

I let out my guttural moan, and I can imagine Enzo grinning in response.

"Are you getting hot from my touch, baby?"

"Yes," I croon.

"Good. I want you to put your hand under your shirt and gently slide up until you are holding one of your perky breasts that I love."

I do as he says, ignoring the scars on my body as I feel my skin. I gasp when my hand flicks over the nipple.

"You naughty girl, I didn't say you could touch your nipple yet," Enzo says.

My eyes are heavy, and I feel him all around me even though he's not here.

"You make me naughty," I say.

Enzo growls. "Pinch your nipple and tell me much it turns you on."

"I am, and it feels so good."

"Harder."

I pinch harder, and I think I could come from playing with my nipples alone. I haven't touched myself since Enzo left with Milo. This release is long overdue.

"Fuck, Enzo, I'm—"

"Come, beautiful."

His voice sends me over the edge.

Jesus, what's wrong with me?

I pant heavily after my release, exhausted but needing more.

"Are you ready for more?"

"Yes, but I want you to come with me this time."

"Oh, I will. Unbutton your pants."

I do. "Unbutton yours, too."

"Way ahead of you."

I imagine Enzo naked, strutting toward me with all of his muscles and scars. But then I remember his shoulders.

"Enzo?"

"Shh, put your fingers under your panties, I'm already gripping my cock, and I want to wait for you."

I quiet my thoughts and put my fingers beneath my panties.

"How wet are you?"

"Soaked, so ready for your cock."

"Shit. You are going to make me come with just your mouth."

I bite my lip. "That's the plan."

I feel him suck in a deep breath through the door.

"I want to watch you pleasure yourself, beautiful. Find that swollen pink clit and tell me how you touch yourself."

I listen carefully to his voice as I move two fingers over my clit. Rubbing in slow lazy circles as I spread my moisture over it.

"God, you're so beautiful," Enzo says as I touch myself.

"And your cock is so thick, long, and veiny."

"It's so ready to sink into you."

"Then do it already."

My heart clenches at how badly I need him to actually push into me. I need the connection we share when his body becomes part of mine. But all I get tonight is his voice, and tonight it will be enough.

"Push a finger inside your tight pussy for me," Enzo says.

I do, and it feels nothing like Enzo inside me.

"Now add another finger."

I do, but it's still not enough.

"How does it feel?"

"Nothing compared to you."

"Add one more finger, baby."

I do, and it's as close as I will get to Enzo. I thrust in and out of my pussy while my other hand massages my clit.

"Faster, beautiful."

I move my fingers faster in and out of my cunt, imagining it's Enzo's cock. I thrust faster and faster, matching his speed.

"Yes, baby, just like that."

"Jesus, Enzo," I cry feeling my body so close to coming.

"Hold on, wait for me," he moans back.

I do, I wait. And in that single moment of waiting, I let all of my emotions flood me. The love. The pain. The worry. The fear. The anxiety. The anger.

It all swirls inside my body, filling every space between

my bones. Taking root as one emotion—fucking love. The kind of love that is powerful and unrelenting.

Before tonight, I had given up on trying to save Enzo. I had given up on saving the Black empire from falling into the wrong hands, but Enzo restored my love for him with one orgasm.

"Come for me, Kai," Enzo says, his voice strained. I know he's about to pour his load out all over the dirty floor.

"Enzo!" I cry.

"Kai!" Enzo growls.

The orgasm lasts forever and not long enough. Because the moment feels like it could sustain me forever, but when it's over, I can't live without that feeling again.

We don't speak, knowing the second we speak ends our fantasy. We will return to reality. To worries and anxieties about what is to come.

So we let the ecstasy last as long as possible. I redress after a few minutes with the scent of Enzo hanging in the air between us.

"How are your shoulders feeling now?" I finally ask, when I know our time is almost up. They must ache like a motherfucker.

"They feel good."

"Liar."

"How does your shoulder feel?" he asks about the cut Milo made in my shoulder.

"It feels like a tiny cut not worth addressing."

"I'm sorry. If I could have chosen anyone else, anyone other than Milo, I would have."

"I know. I just don't know how either one of us is going to survive this. I can't watch you in pain."

"I can't either."

"Fuck, I hate my father so much."

"Our fathers came up with the most twisted, fucked up games."

We both sigh, silently cursing our fathers and families for creating this stupid contest. The challenge was meant to keep the strongest in power. It was meant to ensure that Black never lost the ultimate power we hold. But our families fucked up. The empire is about to fall into the hands of our enemy.

"How about you surrender after this round? Put us both out of our misery," Enzo says.

"How about you surrender?" I respond.

"Another round of truth or lies to determine who surrenders?" Enzo pleads, thinking it's his only chance to get me to quit first.

A tear drips down my cheek. *Thank God he can't see me, or he'd see how close I am to cracking and stopping this game now.* Because I can't watch Enzo get hurt.

I shake my head but don't answer him. He doesn't prod me to play or speak again. We both just enjoy the silence and hope the other survives longer than we do. Because neither of us wants to be the one who survives and is forced to live without the other.

And if Enzo stays with Milo, that's exactly what's going to happen.

I wish this game could be decided with a simple game of truth or lies; it would be so much easier to handle. Even though that game hasn't always been kind to me, I always faced the truth with Enzo by my side.

Now, I have to decide what is my own truth. *Can I watch Enzo be tortured? Can I handle his pain at seeing me be tortured? Can I find a way to save him?*

12

ENZO

LISTENING to Kai come at the sound of my voice was up there with the most erotic nights of my life. The round was meant to be torture, and it was, but not because I was kept in a dark cage all night. It was torture to be so close to Kai and yet not be able to touch her.

There was a time when Kai wouldn't let me touch her, and I thought that was pain. But now that I love her, not feeling her is like losing a limb. I don't feel whole without her.

In some ways though, I wish last night had lasted longer. It was torture, but not as much as today will be. Kai was safe as long as we were both locked in our cells. But now I hear the footsteps nearing. Now I know the real suffering is about to begin.

Now is my last moment alone with Kai to tell her whatever she needs to get through today. I can remind her of how strong she is. Tell her how much I've missed her, how I would die for her. Even that I love her.

But I can't say any of those things. I can't say I love you for the first time through a wall.

And Kai must feel that the time for emotions has long gone, because she doesn't tell me she loves me either, even though she's said it before. Instead, she says, "I know. We are ready. Let's do this."

Fuck, so strong, even in the light of darkness.

Our doors are opened simultaneously as the light of the hallway pours inside. But neither of blink or adjust to the light. We are both so used to the light finding us in the darkest of places.

"Time for round two. And we have all agreed it is best to continue the rounds down here. Less messy that way," Archard says, clearing his throat like he is talking about the weather and not about the blood that will soon be pouring from our bodies.

My eyes connect with Kai's in the light of day as we step out of the cages and for a second, I see the heaviness of the night before returning to warrior mode. She's not going to make this easy for me to win.

"Let's start with the cuts before the second round," Archard says looking at Langston.

He approaches me with the knife low in his hand, knowing the anticipation is worse than the actual cut. He inserts the knife into my other thigh, quickly driving the knife in and out.

I make eye contact with Kai as Milo approaches her and I know it's a mistake to watch her. I know the pain of the knife is nothing, but I hate myself for letting him touch her.

Milo stares at her, and I see the disgust she feels for the man. He grabs her shoulders roughly, knowing her left shoulder is still hurt from where he pushed the blade in before. He takes his time, bringing the knife gently to her lips.

If he stabs her lips or anywhere in the face, I'm going to kill him. Right here, right now.

But he doesn't. He trails the blade from her lip, over her chin, and down her neck. Drawing out every motion of the blade until, despite her best effort, there is a tinge of fear in her eyes. Only when he sees it does he drive the knife hard and deep into her other shoulder.

And then she has a gash on each shoulder, matching my bullet wounds.

Kai doesn't react as Milo steps back.

"What is the next game?" Kai asks, impatient and obviously wanting to get as far away from Milo as possible.

Archard nods and brings up the sheet of paper he's been reading the rules from. The list is long and covers multiple pages. *We are in for a long day.*

"Each player is to have one tooth extracted of the tormentor's choosing using these," Archard says, holding up what looks like pliers.

I moan, but not because this is going to hurt too badly. Teeth extraction seems pretty low on a list of torture. But I don't want to put Kai through that pain. And with how twisted Milo is, I wouldn't put it past him to choose one of her front teeth. While it would probably be less painful because there are fewer roots in the front teeth, she would forever look disfigured.

"Enzo is up first," Archard says, holding the pliers up to Langston.

Langston takes them and spins them in his hand casually. He looks over at the chair in the corner of the room. "Take a seat."

I sit down in the chair as Langston approaches.

"Do I need to restrain you?" he asks with a laugh.

"No, but payback is a bitch."

Langston chuckles and then grabs my jaw, opening it, as he decides which tooth to pull. "You don't get to retaliate when I'm doing what you ask and keeping Kai safe. And unfortunately, that means extracting as much pain from you as quickly as possible. Because the only way she will surrender and save herself is if she thinks you are in too much pain to handle any more. So you better sell the pain and agony and not act like you are above it."

"This is for the black eye you gave me in the eighth grade," Langston says louder so everyone can hear. He puts the pliers into my mouth, reaching all the way to the back to grab a molar, and then he tugs.

I moan loudly as soon as he touches the tooth. I grip the handlebars and stomp my feet like he's torturing me, but honestly, I can barely feel the pressure in my mouth.

He twists sharply, breaking one of the roots off from my gums. I can hear the loud crunch, but I might as well have anesthesia pumping through my body. That's how little this hurts.

I glance over at Milo, and I see the glint in his eyes. He injected me with more drugs. *Fuck, how did I not notice him inject me again?* He must have done it when we were first let out of the cells.

It's cheating, but if I say anything Kai is dead. And it's not breaking the rules anyway; there are no rules. There is no such thing as cheating.

I try my best to keep up the act that Langston is torturing me as he continues to break each root free slowly and methodically. And then he finally jerks the tooth free. But all that is left of the pain is the blood oozing in my mouth and the sweat on Langston's brow. He may have pretended he wanted to torture me, but he hated it.

I glance over at Kai, who is frowning. She's not buying

my pained and tortured act. Her eyes flick up at Langston with a struggling expression on her face as if to say—*I thought you were on my side. And torturing the man I love isn't doing that.*

Langston doesn't apologize, though. He was never one to apologize for doing what he thought was right. And I don't blame him; he should never apologize for protecting Kai.

"My turn," Milo says, walking to Langston to grab the pliers.

Milo grabs them before Langston even has time to wipe off the blood. I know it won't freak Kai out to taste my blood, but it would make me feel better if he did it.

Kai doesn't look at Milo or the pliers, and I know where she's going. I can see her mind shutting me out. Her heart turning colder, locking itself in its cage. I don't think she will completely shut herself away, at least not to complete this round, but if the rounds keep getting harder, she might eventually shut it all off, shut me out, and then she will be unstoppable. With her feelings shut off, she won't be able to feel anything, including the torment. She'll play fearlessly and ruthlessly, no matter what. I will have to stop her if I don't want her to get seriously hurt.

"Let's go, bitch," Milo says, pushing her toward the chair.

I jump up. I'm not going to deal with this. I walk straight to Milo, and I punch him hard in the face. I hear the snap of his jaw and witness blood bust free from his lip.

I wait for the inevitable blow I'm about to receive back, but when Milo gathers himself, he just laughs at my reaction, like he was purposefully goading me on to show Kai how far I'll go to save her. And that she just needs to give up now.

"You treat her with respect, or I'll end you and our deal. Do you understand me?"

Milo twirls the pliers in his hand, continuing to laugh. But I see everyone else's faces in the room—Archard's, Langston's, Liesel's. They all look horrified and in awe of what I just did. And I know it's not the punch causing them to look like this. It's the look on my own face. The anger pulsing through my veins has them scared. Because when I get this way, there is no telling what is going to happen next.

Kai doesn't even register the exchange. She's gone to her safe place—and that scares me just as much, because as much as my body is pumped filled with narcotics to keep me from feeling any pain, her body has shut off all her nerve receptors. She won't feel anything either.

"Take a seat," Milo says to Kai.

She looks at him with a blank expression and starts walking to the chair. She brushes past me, and I let my fingertips brush against hers, hoping the tingling feeling will melt some of the cold walls she put up.

When I touch her, she finally looks at me. But instead of a smile, I get a glare—dark, brooding, and pained.

I reluctantly step out of her way. Liesel comes over to stand next to me; I assume to offer me support as I watch the woman I love be tortured by a madman.

Kai takes a seat, and the blood in my veins is fire—I'm going to burn from the inside out.

"Open your mouth," Milo says, with a cocky grin.

She opens automatically, but her eyes tell me she isn't here.

And in that moment, I'm happy. I don't want her to feel fear or pain. Keep it turned off.

I take a deep breath and close my eyes as Milo hovers over Kai. I can't watch this. I can't watch him touch her without killing him right now and dooming us all. Because one thing I learned while captured by Milo is he has allies. Ones that would avenge his death in an instant. And he has a number two to take his place, but I don't know who he is yet.

"You don't get to close your eyes," Liesel says next to me.

My eyes fly open. "It's the only way I can get through this."

"No, it's not, and you know it. Keep your damn eyes open."

I turn toward Kai and watch as Milo inserts the pliers and begins to pull. I expect for her to react, but she doesn't. I don't know how she turns her ability to feel off like that, but it's both a gift and curse. I just hope she can find herself again when this is all over.

He pulls and jerks. I wince and the whole room gasps at the sight of the blood filling her mouth. But she doesn't even squeeze the armrests of the chair. She's as calm as if she were sitting there drinking coffee.

"You don't deserve her," Liesel says, crossing her arms as she glares at me.

"I know."

"Then save her; set her free."

"I can't do that. This is me setting her free."

Liesel shakes her head. "You're an idiot. You know that, right?"

"Fuck off, Liesel."

She smiles. "I'm going to enjoy her torturing you. Because my money is on you breaking long before she does."

13

KAI

I feel nothing.

Not the pull of my tooth.

Not the menacing touch from Milo as he grabs my jaw.

Not the look from Enzo begging me to stop.

Nothing.

At least until I taste the blood. The blood wakes me up and reminds me of what is at stake.

My life.

Enzo's life.

And the lives of everyone who works for Black or has come to need the empire for protection.

I spit out the blood onto the floor and then get the hell out of the chair before Milo decides the trauma wasn't enough and he needs to pull another tooth.

The fog lifts a little, and I look over at Enzo who looks white with rage. *You can stop this. Just say the word, and all of this ends,* I send to him.

And then I spot Liesel. She might be the only one truly on my side, but I don't know what her motivations are.

Milo wants to destroy me.

Enzo wants to save me.

Langston wants to protect me.

And Liesel wants me to kick all of these guys' asses. I can tell from the smirk and wink she gives me when I get out of the chair.

I can win this, I know I can, but at what cost?

And is winning going to actually help me? I have no idea. But I will keep playing until I know the answer.

I know that getting a tooth pulled hurts. I remember back to when I was ten and had to have a tooth pulled. Dad pulled it because it had a cavity, and we supposedly couldn't afford a dentist. It was a baby tooth, but it still hurt like a motherfucker since it wasn't loose.

Getting a permanent tooth pulled hurts.

The amount of blood and swelling in my mouth should be enough to clue me into the pain, even though I barely feel anything.

But Enzo didn't feel anything either. He may have pretended to cry and wail like a baby, but that's not him. He has a silent power to him. If he felt the pain, he would internalize it so only I would feel it with him. He wouldn't vocalize his pain until he'd been tortured for hours and needed a release.

Something is going on, and I'm not the only one who notices it. But this game comes with no rules. So whatever Enzo's secret to feeling nothing is, it doesn't matter, because it won't change anything.

"Would anyone like to surrender before the next round starts?" Archard asks, looking between Enzo and me.

I spit out more blood—the iron taste oozing over my tongue. *God, I hate the taste of blood.*

I glare at Archard for even asking me if I am going to surrender. I surrendered to let Milo take Enzo; I'm not going to give up again.

Enzo growls at Archard.

Archard rubs his neck. "Sorry for asking." He looks at Milo, and I know it's my turn to get cut.

I brace myself for Milo's touch more than for the cut of the knife. Last round he took a torturously long time. I can't handle that again.

This time though, that's not on Milo's agenda. He walks up to me with the knife at his side. I try not to pay it any attention as he walks, but my eyes dart down to the shiny metal still covered in mine and Enzo's blood from the last time.

Milo grabs my shoulder, and unlike Enzo's touch that burns in the best possible way, his touch electrocutes me making me powerless to what he's going to do next. And then I feel the jab of the knife into my stomach, taking my breath away.

I cough from the sudden intrusion and look down at the knife still in my body. Somehow it feels like the knife doubled in size since the last time, but I know the sudden sharp pain is just from where he stabbed me and how forcefully he did it.

Milo grins at my reaction as I cough again, trying to regain my breath before he removes the knife. He spins it around, my blood flinging from the edge. He then tosses it at Langston who catches it expertly as he stands next to Enzo.

Langston gives Enzo no warning as he thrusts the knife into his stomach in the same way Milo did to me. It has the same effect on Enzo as it did to me. It knocks the wind from

Enzo's lungs. Langston is done playing around. He wants this over as much as Milo does.

"This is the third round and will involve water," Archard says. He pulls out his phone, texts someone, and two men enter with a large vat of water.

Fuck you, father. Fuck you. When I'm finished with these stupid games, I'm going to hunt him down and kill him. I don't care if I promised that he could live. I want him dead for coming up with such twisted games.

"Your head will be held under the water three times, each time longer than the first. I won't tell you how long you will be held under, but I will time you and signal to your tormentor when the time is up. Kai, you will go first. If you would like to stop at any time, simply hold your hand up," Archard says.

I don't wait for Milo to order me around this time. I walk over to the large trough and kneel in front of it. I hate the water after six years of torment on the ocean. But I've gotten over my fear. Enzo helped me. I can do this. It's all about remaining calm and blocking everything out.

I clear my thoughts and go back to my quiet, calm place.

Milo approaches from behind, and I don't react. I feel his hand on my neck, but the pain is gone. I've shut him out.

"You need to end this, now," Milo says in my ear.

Don't let him goad you. He's just trying to mess with your head.

Sure enough, he plunges my head into the water before I can react. I didn't even have time to take a breath.

And as much as I want to remain calm, I can't because my lungs are burning, already begging for oxygen. I grab the edge of the trough as my body starts flailing, trying to get out of the water—but maybe I need to react? I need

Enzo to stop this game. And he only will if he sees me in pain.

So I let the pain swoop over me. I let myself feel. And for once, I don't hate it. Because it sparks my rage, and I know that feeling this way is what it's going to take to find a way out of this mess.

My mouth opens, and I inhale some of the water in a search for air. All of the work Enzo did to help me get over the fear of the water is going to come raging back after this.

My lungs begin to fill with water instead of oxygen, and I'm afraid whatever ridiculous amount of time my father set for this task is going to be too much. I'm going to drown.

But just as I don't think I can take it anymore, my head is released, and I'm out of the confines of the water.

I cough violently, water expelling from my lungs. I can feel Enzo's eyes on me, and then he races over to comfort me.

I put up a hand, stopping Enzo. I don't want his comfort right now.

Enzo stops in his tracks. "Are you okay, Kai?"

I don't answer. I am anything but okay. But it's not enough for me to surrender and lose the game.

I feel Milo's hands on my neck, and this time, I'm more prepared for it. I take a deep breath just before my head plunges under. The first few seconds are easier this time as I have a reserve of oxygen to keep me calm.

But then the familiar panic of my lungs washes over me again. And again, I let it. Enzo was already beginning to crack. And although the panic sucks, I know this time I'm going to live. I'm not going to stay under so long that I'm going to drown. I'm going to survive this. So even though my lungs panic, my mind doesn't.

My head feels the air again, and I cough up the water

that snuck in. But before I can register anything, my head plunges under again.

More pain.

More panic.

More anxiety.

Longer and longer my head is under the water. But I feel like I could do this all day. And this is the last time.

The last time seems like the shortest, even though I was told it was the longest.

And when I break for the surface again, I suck in a deep breath of oxygen without having to cough this time. As if each time I was under my body adjusted more and more to the water.

I stare down at the water in front of me. *You are not my enemy. The man gripping my hair is.*

I stand up, and Liesel tosses me a towel that I begin to dry off with.

I look at Enzo who is panicked, but not for his turn, for me.

I wink at him. "I hope you have a good pair of lungs on you."

Enzo's face softens a little, and I don't know why I made this easier on him.

Langston and Enzo take Milo and my's place as I stand next to Liesel trying to dry off and remove the memories of being underwater from my brain.

But when Langston pushes Enzo's head under, I freak out as I watch his calm turn to panic.

"It wasn't that bad when you were in the water. Remember how it felt. Enzo has this," comes Liesel's calm voice.

I clinch the towel to my face, not sure if he's going to survive the dunking in the water.

"He's going to drown. I have to stop this," I whisper.

"No, he's not. He thought the same thing watching you. But the time goes by quickly. It's harder to watch than to go through it," Liesel tries to reassure me.

Finally, on Archard's signal, Langston lets Enzo's head up.

"God, I can't do this two more times," I say, feeling tears threaten.

"You are a badass. Don't you dare lose because you can't watch your man get a little wet," Liesel whispers so only I can hear in her strongest voice.

Enzo coughs and then his head goes back under.

I count to myself trying to distract myself.

One.

Two.

Three.

When I get to a hundred, I lose it.

I start pacing, unable to watch anymore.

Milo smirks, thinking I'm going to lose on this round.

"Fuck you," I curse, not caring that by showing him how this is affecting me he's winning.

"Gladly," he says back.

I tug at my hair to keep from killing him.

And then I hear Enzo's breath as his lungs fill with air when Langston lets him up. *Only one more.* Enzo can do this. I can do this.

Langston barely lets Enzo catch his breath before he shoves him underwater again. And this time I feel it all.

Enzo's lungs fill with water this time, as he didn't take a good breath before going under. They burn despite whatever is pumping through his veins to keep the pain away. The feel of his lungs panicking overrides the drugs. Trying to tell him to reach the surface and breathe. But Enzo doesn't have any say in the matter.

Just stay calm. It's almost over.

But Enzo can't stay calm. Not when he's running out of his precious oxygen. His legs tremble, and his arms push against the edge, trying to break free of Langston's hold. But Langston holds him firm, watching Archard intently for the signal, and I feel Langston's panic too. He's not so sure Enzo has this.

I feel Enzo's heart beating quickly, racing to try to spread what little oxygen he has through his body.

I bite my lip to keep from screaming as I stare at Archard, but I know he still has several seconds left.

Come on, Enzo. Relax. Let go.

Finally, after what feels like hours, Archard gives the signal. Langston doesn't just let go this time; he jerks Enzo up by the back of his shirt. Enzo falls lifeless to the floor.

I run to him, but Liesel grabs me to keep me from being consumed with the pain.

"Help him!" I scream.

Langston kneels down and starts performing CPR. He pushes hard on his chest, but Enzo doesn't move.

My hands go over my face as I watch him. He can't drown. He can't die.

But Enzo Black is human, just like all of us. And in this moment, I've never realized just how human he really is.

"Dammit, fucking cough," Langston says, pushing harder on his chest.

Enzo finally coughs up the water, and I see his lungs rise and fall.

Langston sits back on his ankles. "Thank fuck."

I let the tear I've been holding in loose. And Enzo's eyes

go straight to the tear. I don't know who got hurt worse with him almost drowning—him or me.

But this stupid round got to us in a way the previous rounds didn't. And I don't think my heart can last too many more.

14

ENZO

I DON'T KNOW what happened. I must have blacked out. And I woke up with Langston pressing hard on my chest and Kai's voice screaming with tears in her eyes.

Fuck, I have to get my shit together if I'm going to survive this game.

Langston puts his hand out, and I take it slowly, getting up.

Liesel tosses me a towel with a scowl, obviously thinking my almost death moment was an act like the previous round. It wasn't. I just lost focus and passed out. But as much as I want to win, I won't lose control like that again.

I dry my hair and face off, trying to recompose myself before looking at Kai again. She looks like she can't decide between killing and fucking me.

Fuck my life. Why can't I just have a normal life where when a woman wants to fuck me, I get to fuck her?

Archard clears his throat and then hands the knife to Langston to start the next round. *Fuck that stupid knife.* The first few times were painless, but the longer this goes, the more the drugs are going to wear out of my system.

Langston goes easy on me this time though, barely slicing my bicep, and I don't feel a thing. My eyes are still focused on Kai and her worried face.

End this. Please, I can't watch you suffer.

Langston tosses the knife hard to Milo, who barely avoids it crashing into his body. Instead, it bounces on the floor before he picks it up.

Go easy on her, I plead. Her shield is down from watching me almost drown.

But of course, he doesn't. He stabs her in the chest right over her heart. Thank God the blade is too short to reach her heart and do any real damage.

But she gasps, and her face twists—the stabbing amplifies the pain she's already feeling in her heart. She sucks in air, trying to breathe through the pain, but a low moan escapes her throat.

Fuck me.

I can't watch this.

Milo finally pulls the knife out, and I have to look away to keep from throwing her over my shoulder and getting her the hell out of here.

"This round is simple," Archard starts.

Shit, nothing about this is simple.

"Your shoulder is to be dislocated."

I sigh—*easy my ass.*

I've had my shoulder dislocated before. Not when I was expecting it, but in the heat of a fight. The pain will rip through you, but it's the pain of putting it back that hurts worse.

Worst of all, it's a physical act. Milo is going to have to touch Kai to dislocate her shoulder. I'm going to have to watch him break her. And I don't know if I can.

Kai notices my hesitation and raises an eyebrow as if to

say if you're going to bow out, do it before you have your shoulder dislocated you idiot. But then, I've never been very smart.

Langston walks over to me and gives me one look to prepare me. Fuck, this is going to hurt like hell because of the wound in both of my shoulders. It doesn't matter which one he dislocates.

I close my eyes and tense my body as he grabs my left wrist and throws it behind my body, applying just the right amount of pressure. We've tortured men before and know exactly how to dislocate a shoulder.

With one quick pop, my shoulder is out.

But I don't feel a damn thing—*fucking drugs*. I should be in tears or cursing up a storm right now. I should be making Kai worried for me. This blow, after almost drowning, would have been enough to break her. Instead, I can't even fake being in pain.

Langston looks to Archard, "When can I pop it back in place?"

"When the game is over."

I hold my dislocated left shoulder loosely in my right arm, knowing if it's still dislocated when the drugs wear off it's going to hurt like a motherfucker.

And then I look at Kai, trying to decide if I'm going to let her go through the pain.

She just winks at me. She's had her shoulder dislocated before.

I shake my head. *Of course, she has.* She's been through more pain than anything else.

Milo grabs her right arm, her dominant hand—the fucker. And then he takes his time examining it, holding it in his hands as if he's never dislocated a shoulder before and doesn't know how it's done.

Liesel crosses her arms and stares right at me. She wants me to end this. But I think Kai would kill me for ending this on something easy. She can handle this like the warrior she is.

It's me who is weak. Kai is my weakness. And I'm not afraid to show it.

"Stop messing around and do it already. Kai's not fazed by your antics. She's stronger than you realize," I say to Milo.

Milo growls and then throws her arm back.

The pop is audible for everyone in the room to hear.

I wince as I stare at Kai, but she just smiles like he cracked her knuckles and not her shoulder.

When he releases her, she cracks her neck side to side in an amused sort of way.

And damn if I don't get hard watching how much of a badass she is. Why I ever thought she wasn't strong enough to be Black is beyond me. She's the strongest person in this room. And my heart is hers completely.

15

KAI

GOD, *my shoulder stings.* But I'm not going to let this room filled with men know that. They all look at me with predatory eyes, just waiting for me to show how much of an easy prey I am. But they are sadly mistaken if they think I'm going to show a second of weakness.

I don't even let myself cradle my arm. *No weakness.* I feel like a great warrior about to end a battle.

Enzo is strong, so this fight could last forever. But I won't let it. This game was built for me. My father designed a twisted game and then prepared me in the worst way for it. Enzo's father was evil, but he has nothing on my sick father.

"Knife," I say to Archard. I'm tired of waiting. I want this game over.

Archard hands me the knife which I point over my heart. "Going to stab me in the heart again?" I ask Milo, trying my best to sound threatening. This game is as much psychological as it is physical.

Milo takes the knife, presses it close to my heart, but then at the last minute stabs me in the back.

I laugh, not feeling a damn thing. "You would be the kind of man who would stab me in the back."

"And you are the kind of woman who is going to look good lying on her back while I fuck you," Milo says, so low only I can hear.

I growl. "Never going to happen."

"We will see," Milo says, looking from me to Enzo.

Langston grabs the knife from Milo and jabs it into Enzo's dislocated shoulder.

"Good," Archard says, satisfied with the preliminary cuts. I think the sick bastard is enjoying it, until he coughs, struggling to get the next words out.

Archard goes to his bag and produces a hammer, and I know this is when the real battle begins. He hands the hammer to Milo.

"Three hits with this," Archard says.

"No!" Enzo screams.

"Are you giving up?" Archard asks.

Langston looks Enzo dead in the eye. *Of course, Langston is on Enzo's side.* He thinks if I win, it will be more tempting for Milo to trade me for Enzo. Langston grabs his shoulders and turns Enzo away, and I know if I whimper, if I let the pain in, I could win. But I don't want to win by default. I want to win because I've earned it.

"Do your worst," I way to Milo.

He grabs the hammer and hits me hard in the chest. I'm knocked backward. My ribs shatter beneath the floor.

I don't bother to get up. The floor will be my home for the next two hits.

But I shut it all out and go to my happy place. I'm back in the dungeon with Enzo whispering my name on his breath, only this time his arms are around me. His lips pressing against mine. His tongue stroking mine. His hands brushing against my face.

I feel warm and safe. His arms wrap around me...*wait*.

My eyes fly open, and I realize Enzo does have his arms wrapped around me as tears fill his eyes.

I smile up at him, and the tears burst from his eyes.

"God, how are you so strong? I'm so sorry, forgive me," Enzo says, his voice wavering.

"There is nothing to forgive. I don't feel anything."

Enzo shakes his head as tears drip down his cheeks and onto mine.

"Is it over?" I ask.

"Soon, baby. Really, soon. I promise," Enzo sets me down gently on the floor, and Liesel takes my head in her lap as Enzo reluctantly walks away from me.

"What happened?" I ask, my voice weak.

"Milo hit you more than three times. He got carried away. Enzo attacked and got him to stop. You though—you looked serene. Like you were somewhere else through it all."

"I was," I smile.

"Good. You are going to win, no way Enzo allows that to happen again."

"What happens since Milo broke the rules?"

I look over at a bloodied Milo.

Liesel shrugs. "Archard allowed Enzo to beat the crap out of him and comfort you. I don't know how else he can make it fair. The damage has already been done."

I continue to rest my head as Langston takes the hammer. Usually, I would be worried Langston was about to do some real damage to Enzo, but I know after what Milo did to me, Langston could try to hammer Enzo to the ground, and he wouldn't even feel it. Forget about the drugs already soothing his veins. This new rage Enzo feels is consuming everything in his body.

I barely notice as Langston hits Enzo because my eyes stay on Enzo's face. His eyes are glued to mine, and he doesn't grimace or even move as each powerful hit is delivered. He's a rock, one very pissed off rock, and he's ready to get his revenge.

Langston stops, dropping the hammer, and I examine Enzo's body for any signs of injury, but I find none. I don't think Langston put all of his strength behind the hits. He looks over at me as concerned as Enzo was.

Enzo looks right at me and says, "This ends, now."

I brush my bloodied hair from my face with my left hand. My right shoulder is dislocated, my lungs are shattered, my shin is most likely broken. I'm a mess, but none of those injuries bother me. Not like how I know my heart will break again when Enzo leaves with Milo until the next game.

I need this to end. I need Enzo to be safe, but I won't be the one to end it.

"Help me, Liesel. Help me. I can't let Enzo win," I whisper into her lap.

"He won't win, not in the end," Liesel says.

"But we will save him, right? In the end?" My voice is heavy as my eyes grow foggy. My body can't handle too many more rounds of this.

"Yes, stingray, we will save him." My eyes drift closed, and I don't know if I was listening to Liesel's voice or Zeke's.

16

ENZO

I AM NOT WAITING. I will kill Milo Wallace. As soon as he gets me back to Italy. I will kill him.

I don't care how many of his enemies will come for me. I will take down every single one. I don't care who is second in command is, I'll kill him too.

I'll make Langston take Kai far away, where no one can find her. Maybe Alaska or Nebraska or something, no one would ever look for her there.

But I can't let what Milo did go unpunished.

He could have killed Kai.

How stupid was I to think the only way to save her was to take a deal with this monster?

It was still a good plan. I got more information on the inside than I could ever get on the outside. I'm prepared to take Milo down now.

But in order for me to get to Milo, this game needs to end. And I have to win. I can't risk Kai winning and Milo thinking she's the better competitor. I can't risk him trading me for her.

He will never touch her.

Archard hands Langston the knife to start the next round—the final round if I have it my way.

"End this," I command Langston.

I need him to hurt me so much this round Kai won't have a choice but to surrender.

Langston twirls the knife, considering his move. He gives me a warning look as his lips tighten.

I don't brace myself for the cut. I look over at Kai still lying on Liesel's lap on the floor. Whatever pain I'm about to experience is for her. To save her.

And then Langston jabs the knife into my throat.

My eyes water at the sudden intrusion. Then Langston breaks the rules: he lets the knife slip and cuts my carotid artery.

The blood starts spirting, and I feel cold instantly.

I don't have much time. Maybe only a few minutes before I pass out if I'm lucky and the cut isn't too deep. Somehow I remain standing.

It was a risky move on Langston's part. But I'd rather die and keep Kai safe, than stay alive to watch her be taken.

Although, if I die, Langston is the only person left to keep Kai safe.

So I can't die. I trust Langston with my life, but not with Kai's. Kai is mine to protect, to save, to love.

"No!" Kai screams when she realizes what Langston did.

She scrambles off Liesel's lap. Her injured leg and dislocated shoulder do nothing to stop her from getting to me.

But then Milo moves into her path.

"Move," she says, with a tear-stained face.

"Not until you surrender. Or should I give you the same treatment with the knife?" Milo asks.

Kai looks directly at me with so much pain dripping from her eyes. "I surrender."

She shoves Milo out of her way and then grabs my neck. "Get a doctor, now," she looks at Langston.

He presses a button on the wall, and doctor Patten runs down the stairs.

"Fuck," he says, as I fall to the ground and he reaches for my wound. My eyes grow heavy, and the images of Kai get fuzzy.

"He doesn't even feel that...why?" the doctor asks as he presses into his neck.

"I think he pumped him full of drugs," Kai answers and points at Milo.

"What kind?" the doctor asks Milo.

"What fucking kind?" Dr. Patten repeats.

Milo mumbles something back, and then the doctor is looking at me. "The drugs may have just saved your life."

Kai gasps when she hears him say Milo's actions saved my life. I feel really weak, I feel cold like her, and I want to tell her that I'm not saved yet. I could still die.

If I died, she might just kill Milo herself. And then Langston would hide her away. The Black empire would finally fall, but that doesn't matter as long as she's safe.

She grabs my hand in hers and squeezes hard, realizing just how cold I am.

She stops crying, trying to focus on feeling me. On feeling how much I'm here or not with her.

"Enzo, don't you dare die. You haven't even given me a chance to convince you are in love with me," she sobs, kissing my hand.

"I—"

"Shh," she strokes my face.

I already love you. But I realize now isn't the time to say it. If she thinks I love her back, she would never let me go.

"I need to pump some blood into him," the doctor says.

"Go get the blood, asshole," Liesel says to Langston.

Langston cringes. "We haven't restocked after—"

"You fucking idiot! Then why did you slice open his neck and spill his blood everywhere if you weren't sure how to replace it?"

Kai's eyes look at the doctor, and I know he's worried.

"Then we need to get him to a hospital, immediately," the doctor says.

"What about my blood?" Kai asks.

The doctor freezes. "If you or anyone else is a match, then yes, I could use your blood. What is your blood type?"

"O negative."

He smiles. "Give me your arm."

Kai immediately sticks out his arm.

"Is her blood a match?" Langston asks.

"Type O is a universal donor. Anyone can receive her blood." The doctor pulls out a needle and shoves it into Kai's arm. He connects it with a tube and then pushes a different needle through my arm. I watch as the blood leaves her body and travels through the tube to my arm.

Our eyes meet. I have her heart; now I'll have her blood. She's every part of me that matters—*all the good.*

She kisses my forehead gently as more of her blood pours into my body.

"How do you feel?" the doctor asks.

"Cold," I say.

He frowns.

"And happy, and content, and so much more."

The doctor's eyes flicker to Kai's. "I always run cold; I assume my blood does too."

The doctor touches Kai's skin, and she doesn't flinch. He nods understanding when he feels how cold she is.

We all stay silent as more of her blood drips into my body.

Even Milo stays silent. I assume he would be giving orders to get me the hell away from here as soon as possible to protect his asset.

But he doesn't say anything.

Eventually, the doctor checks my pulse and blood pressure again, and the look of relief on his face tells me I'm going to make it.

"I think you've gotten enough blood," the doctor says looking at Kai more closely. "And I think I need to check out your girlfriend next."

Kai shakes her head. "I'm fine."

"You are not fine," I say.

She gives me a stern look that says, don't argue with me.

I smile, but it's my job to argue with her.

"I'm going to disconnect this tube now. And then I'll have you moved to a bed to rest, and we can work on your shoulder after you've rested a bit, and I have a chance to check out your girlfriend," the doctor says, reaching to disconnect the tubes connecting us.

"Wait," I say, reaching up to pull Kai's lips down on mine. I may not get to be inside her when I kiss her, but she gets to be inside me, and I won't waste this moment. Our tongues push into each other's mouths, tasting the blood we are both still oozing. It should be the least sexy, unromantic thing, but in some twisted way, it's perfect. This is us. And it gives me the desire to mark her with my blood more often.

Slowly, Kai pulls away, and it feels like a goodbye. But I see Milo out of the corner of my eye. He's not going to take me until he knows for sure I can survive the trip.

"This isn't goodbye, not yet," I say, as I stroke her cheek.

She smiles, weakly.

The doctor removes the tubing.

"I'm going to need help carrying him upstairs," the doctor says.

Langston jumps in. "I can help."

He puts his arms under my good arm and helps me stand, but I'm weak. There is no way I can walk. So instead, Langston scoops me up like I'm his girl.

It causes the room to smile for a second.

"We'll be back for you," Langston says to Kai as he carries me upstairs with the doctor trailing.

My eyes grow heavy and tired as I'm being carried. But my mind is still on Kai. Beautiful, sexy, broken Kai. My love.

Fuck—

It takes a minute for my mind to realize my mistake.

I left her alone with Milo.

17

KAI

TEARS THREATEN my eyes again as my heart aches at watching Enzo be carried up the stairs and away from me.

Goodbye.

My heart breaks and shatters again, causing far more pain than either my dislocated shoulder or broken leg.

How many times am I going to have to say goodbye to Enzo?

At least once more...

He saved my life. He kept me from enduring whatever task my father had planned next and Milo from beating me to a pulp.

Now, I owe him my life.

Milo has a huge army of allies ready to take us down so they can continue on with their twisted way of life. But Langston contacted our allies, and they are ready to fight.

Now is the time to attack. I'm not good at fighting. I don't know how to lead an army, but Enzo does. There are dozens of Milo's men upstairs ready to fire if Milo is touched. He can't be touched here. But I will not let Enzo go back with Milo. Not while he is hurt. Not ever. This is my chance to make the trade. And hope Enzo heals quickly and can gather his army fast.

"Now's your chance," Liesel whispers to me, while pretending to examine my shoulder. She slides me the knife that was used to cut Enzo and me. I slide it in into my sock.

I nod.

"Are you sure about this?" she asks, but I can see the need in her eyes. She may be my friend, but she needs Enzo to be safe.

"Yes," I say.

She squeezes my shoulder tightly. "I'll do what I can to help." And then Liesel runs up the stairs after Langston and Enzo to do what she can to keep them occupied.

That leaves me alone, with Milo.

I use my uninjured arm to push myself up off the ground. Everything hurts. Every little nerve in my body is screaming at me to stop. Every blood vessel is crying for rest. My lungs are burning with sharp shrapnels of my ribs poking them. Not to mention my dislocated shoulder and broken leg.

But none of that matters. Saving Enzo matters. Protecting the Black empire matters. Because without Enzo or the Black empire, women running from men like Milo will never be safe. No one will ever come for them. Enzo is the only man strong enough to face the worst evil, and instead of letting it demolish him, he absorbs it.

"Take me, not him," my voice trembles as I say the words.

Fuck, I'm stronger than this.

Milo cocks his head with his hands in his pants. "What?"

I swallow down the pain. "You heard me. Take me instead of Enzo."

Milo's lips turn upward inching closer to a grin as he stares at me intently. "And why would I do that? You lost, and Enzo did exactly what I told him to do."

"Because you can't take Enzo now. The trip would be too much for his frail body."

Milo's heated gaze, runs up and down my broken body. He wants me more now than ever before. He likes his women broken.

I'm not broken.

"And it wouldn't be too much for your body?"

"No."

His eyes widen.

"It wouldn't be too much. I was held as a captive for six years on a yacht. Beaten every day, but never more. I can survive a few hours in a plane."

He nods. "Maybe you are better adept at traveling right now than your boyfriend is." He licks his bottom lip. "But that doesn't mean I'm going to choose you over him."

"I know who you are," I say out of nowhere—hanging onto any hope of trying to get him to come to my side.

Milo's body stiffens, his chest is held higher, and he stops breathing.

Yes, I'm getting somewhere.

"It doesn't matter who I am."

"I think it does. Does Enzo know? Does he know you are brothers?"

Milo grits his teeth, and his eyes darken.

"That's what I thought. Should I go tell him? Would that change things?"

"It doesn't matter who knows."

It matters, I just don't know why.

Milo starts walking toward the stairwell. I'm running

out of time. If Milo leaves, I can't chase after him. All I have to convince him to take me is my words.

"Take me. Enzo can't change his heir if you take me. He has no children. No closer biological heir to you."

Milo stops walking, his head slowly turning to face me, and I see the heat again as his brain processes what this means for him.

"You can take me, and Enzo will have no choice but to keep his promise to you. He won't have a child if it's not with me," I say.

Milo has turned all the way around, and I see his erection pressing against his zipper.

My stomach churns, *I'm going to be sick.*

"He will attack. He will do anything to get you back."

I cock my head, as I run my tongue over my swollen lip. Trying to look enticing for this sick man. "Does it matter? He attacks, you defeat his armies and show how worthy you are to lead them. And if he doesn't, then you get everything you have ever wanted with no cost to you."

"You're a stupid girl."

Maybe, or maybe I'm brave. Maybe I'm fearless. Maybe I'm in love, and being in love means you will do anything for the other person.

I'm tired of playing games with Milo.

I want him dead.

I'm going to protect Enzo and kill Milo.

Enzo had his chance to kill Milo; he didn't take it. But now he knows everything there is to know about Milo's mansion.

If Milo takes me, Enzo will come. Enzo would have never included me in his plans, but now I'm forcing his hand. Now he has no choice. I'll take Milo down from the inside, and Enzo can attack from the outside. Together we will defeat him.

"I accept your deal. You go with me, and I won't hurt Enzo. And I will remain Enzo's heir to become leader of his empire."

Milo holds out his hand, and reluctantly I put my hand in his, hoping I didn't just give up all of myself in the process.

18

ENZO

MY EYES OPEN, and I feel the pain.

Not the pain in my neck or my shoulder. No, I'm pumped full of enough narcotics to never feel my body again.

No, the pain I feel is the loss of Kai.

She isn't here. I don't feel her anywhere, even before I open my eyes, and my sight confirms it.

Langston is sitting in a chair next to my bed. His head slumped in his hand.

"How long have I been out?" I ask.

He startles, his eyes large as he sees that I'm awake. But he doesn't look happy to see me awake.

"Twenty-four-hours. You've been in a drug-induced coma. The doctor said you needed it to heal after all the blood loss. He was worried you had swelling in your brain and around your heart."

I had swelling in my heart alright, and it's going to get worse after I ask my next question.

"Where is Kai?"

Langston looks at his hands.

"Where the fuck is Kai?" I scream.

"You need to relax. You have a lot of injuries, and I'll explain everything."

"Where is Kai?" my voice waivers as I say it, because I already know the answer. I know why he isn't willing to tell me.

"She went with Milo."

I close my eyes as the agony washes over me in one large wave consuming my entire body. But I don't have time to wallow in my loss. I can't let Milo have her a second longer.

I sit up in the bed and pull off all the chords attached to my chest. And then I grab the IV and rip it from my arm.

Langston doesn't move as I get out of the bed. And then I shove him with everything I have toward the wall. His body hits it, but he doesn't fight me.

Instinctively, I reach behind me for my gun, but I'm in a damn hospital dress. And I don't have a gun on me.

"Looking for a gun to shoot me?" Langston asks his voice heavy.

"Yes, you deserve to feel some pain after you let her go with him. I gave you one job: protect her. At all costs. And the first time she's alone with Milo, you let her go. You have no idea what he will do to her."

I shove harder.

"I have a clue what Milo will do."

Langston reaches behind his back and pulls a gun, but instead of aiming, he hands it to me.

"Take it, use it. I deserve it. I couldn't protect her. I failed." Tears fill his eyes. "I should have been the one who died, instead of Zeke. Zeke would have saved her."

Damn right.

I shove the gun at his chest and feel all of his suffering. It matches my own. *How could Kai have pierced three men's hearts? Three men who didn't have a heart to begin with?*

"Fuck you, Langston." I toss the gun down, knowing I can't shoot him—but I'm still pissed.

As soon as the gun drops, I drive my fist into his jaw.

He takes it, but on the second punch, he automatically starts fighting back. He lands his own hit to my jaw, and then he's slamming me backward. We've fought hundreds of times together since we were kids, and this is just one more of those times.

I get angry. And I need to let off steam. Langston is much the same. And then I explode. Two hotheads together don't mix well. But damn did we learn how to fight together.

And Zeke would be the one to end our fights. Langston and I have similar skills and body sizes, but Zeke was always twice as large as us. If he got involved, the fight would end immediately.

"Stop fighting, you idiots!" Liesel says, stomping into the room.

I have Langston in a headlock, and he's punching my stomach.

We freeze but don't release each other.

She shakes her head at us. She might as well point her finger at us and yell at us like we are her children for how she is looking at us.

"For heaven's sake, let Langston go, Enzo. And Langston, really? You're going to punch Enzo knowing how damaged his body is?"

We both release each other.

It doesn't stop the glare in her eyes. "You don't get to be mad at Langston. If you want to be mad at someone, be mad at me."

"You? What did you do?" I ask.

"I helped Kai save you."

"You what?" I screech.

"Sit, now," Liesel says, pointing to the bed.

I can't sit down. This woman is insufferable. I knew she didn't like Kai, but I didn't think she would stoop to trading her to Milo.

"Sit if you want me to tell you what happened."

Reluctantly, I sit on the edge of the bed.

"You too," she says to Langston.

Langston lowers himself back into the chair he was sitting in before. But the stiff look he's giving Liesel tells me he wasn't privy to whatever she did any more than I am.

"Kai has a plan to end this. And I helped her execute it," Liesel starts.

"There is no ending *this*. Not if she's putting her life at risk."

"Shut up, and let me talk."

I zip my mouth closed, but only because I need to know the truth.

"When you left Kai, you broke her heart. You have no idea how much. You have no idea what that pain is like. You've never loved anyone, but Kai loves stronger than anyone I've ever seen, me included. She couldn't survive without you. Especially knowing that you were hurting and there was something she could do about it."

Please tell me her plan was to blow up Milo's plane before she could step foot on it.

"You left her. You abandoned her. And you made your own stupid plan to protect her without involving her. Without talking to her first. And yes, you protected her, but it didn't matter when you took the most important part of her with you."

Tears are hidden behind Liesel's eyes.

I stare at them. I've never seen Liesel cry. She's too strong, too above that level of weakness. The last time I saw her cry was when I was torturing her. But this, this is from heartbreak. Liesel hurts for Kai.

"So Kai took back her life. And I helped her. And I would suggest when all this is over, you two learn to communicate and trust each other; otherwise, your relationship is doomed to fail."

"And where did you learn that, Dr. Phil?" Langston says.

Liesel growls. "It doesn't matter where I learned it."

"What is your genius plan?" I ask.

Liesel's head pops back in my direction. "You know everything about Milo after spending weeks at his mansion."

"I do." I don't want Kai anywhere near it.

"You were there for weeks, but never had an opportunity to kill him because Milo never let you get close enough."

Fuck, I know where this is going, and I hate this plan.

"Kai, on the other hand, can get close. Very close. Milo thinks she's weak. He'll put his guard down around her."

I feel like I'm suffocating listening to Liesel talk. *I fucking hate this plan.*

"She will kill him. And then you will attack with your men and rescue her."

"I'm not going to use her as a distraction so I can attack while she has Milo occupied."

"You don't have a choice. The plan is already in motion. Milo is too smart. And his mansion is too impenetrable to not have someone on the inside to let you in or at least distract him while you take it."

"He'll be expecting that. As you said, Milo isn't stupid. He'll be waiting for me to attack."

"Maybe, but then Kai will signal when Milo has let his guard down. She will let us know when to attack."

"No, we will attack as soon as we can get there. Within the next few hours, preferably," I say.

"Agreed," Langston says.

Liesel shakes her head. "You know that won't work. Milo will be ready. He won't touch her until he thinks you won't attack."

"This plan won't work."

"It will. It already has."

"What do you mean?"

"It will work, because Kai can communicate with us. She can let us know when to attack. Milo thinks we are weak after his attack."

"Attack?" Langston asks.

I'm sitting on my bed at the beach house. At some point, I must have been moved here. Which means the attack didn't happen here.

"Milo attacked Surrender. He thinks he wiped out most of our men. But only one man was hurt, because Kai was able to warn us. Something you should have considered doing before you let Milo take you," Liesel scolds.

I frown. "And how exactly can she communicate with us?"

Liesel whistles.

The door opens, and a woman I vaguely recognize walks in carrying a laptop.

"Hello Mr. Enzo, I mean Mr. Black, Mr. Rinaldi? I don't know what to call you," the woman says. She's wearing high heels, a black skirt, and a white blouse. But the shoes are too small, and the blouse is too big. Her hair is tied up in a messy bun. She looks a like little girl playing dress up.

"Enzo is fine."

"Enzo, I'm Yolie. I've worked for you for three years since I graduated," Yolie continues.

My eyes cut to Liesel, trying to understand why this stranger is standing in my bedroom when I have much more important things to worry about.

"I work on your security team, developing the latest technologies."

"She's a genius is what she is saying," Liesel says, smiling.

Yolie blushes. "I wouldn't say that. But I did design some earrings for Kai. I figured Milo would be less likely to suspect small diamond stud earrings than a necklace or bracelet."

I stare at her, confused.

"She designed earrings that allow us to track Kai at all times, and Kai can tap out simple messages to us through the earrings. We taught Kai a few letters of Morse code. That's how she let us know there was going to be an attack at Surrender and to get everyone out before the explosion."

"Surrender is destroyed?" I ask.

Liesel nods with a smile.

She hates that place as much as I do. Too many memories of my father haunt those walls. I'm not sad the place is gone; I should have destroyed it long ago.

"Where is Kai now?" I ask, desperate to see Kai and hopeful she is safe.

Yolie starts typing on the computer, and then she shoves the laptop onto my lap.

"She's safe. We are monitoring her location. They just landed in Italy."

I don't want to know what took them so long to get to Italy. But Kai is anything but safe.

"She can send a distress call with a long press of the

earrings. Or if they are removed, we are notified and have a team already in Italy ready to move in. But we could really use you, boss. You know the compound better than anyone since you've lived there. Kai is going to try to find a way to let us in undetected, but if not, it's all up to you."

I look at Langston who has already hopped up and most likely already knows what I'm about to say.

"Get my damn plane ready. We are going to Italy."

Liesel crosses her arms. "You will wait for Kai's signal. We can tell if she's distressed. If he touches her, we will know. The earrings detect changes in heart rate."

I stand up, coming eye to eye with Liesel. "If I get a chance to take out Milo, I'm going to take it. I'm not waiting on some signal. Kai isn't the only person on the inside I can trust."

"Just promise me you won't trade yourself to save Kai," Liesel begs.

"I can't do that."

She shakes her head. "You love her."

I don't answer.

"Jesus, I never thought I'd say you are a good man. I never thought I'd see you in love. And I never thought that love would be the death of you."

I step past Liesel. *I'm coming, Kai. Just don't do anything to get yourself hurt.*

I need to kill Milo. I've wanted to since the first day I met him and saw him look at Kai, but I couldn't because Milo's empire isn't about him. It will survive long after Milo's death. And I don't know who his successor is. I don't know who will come at us after Milo is gone. And that person could be worse than Milo.

I thought I was protecting Kai by trying to keep her out of this fight. But I should have known better.

We love each other. I would give my life for her. The only way to keep her safe and protect that love is to tell her the truth. To be honest and share everything. And then to take down our enemies together. Even if it will kill me to watch her fight by my side.

But every time I've tried to protect her myself, it backfires on me.

I can't keep doing that.

Kai has a plan, and I'll do my best to stick to it. It might be the only way to earn her trust. But even if her plan works, even if we kill Milo and get her out unscathed, I'm not sure it will be enough.

19

KAI

I THINK I hate planes now worse than yachts.

The plane ride lasted forever.

At least that's what it feels like when I don't know if Enzo is alive or dead.

The second I overheard Milo talking about blowing up Surrender, I sent a broken message to Liesel.

But my Morse code isn't the best. And I'm not sure I sent it correctly or not. I'm not sure if Liesel is alive or dead. The same with Enzo and Langston or any of the other loyal men in the club.

My heart feels heavy and disconnected. I would permanently feel numb if Enzo were dead—my connection gone.

He's alive; he has to be.

But that's the problem with these damned earrings. They are helpful, but not enough. I can communicate with them, but they can't communicate with me.

The plane circled overhead of Surrender until it was finished. Milo wanted to watch the explosion. What he was looking for, I don't know, but he seemed happy and satisfied as we flew away. We made one stop to pick up a doctor.

I must have looked pretty pale and weak for Milo to pick up a doctor to help me.

But all the doctor did was give me some blood through an IV in my arm. He didn't set my dislocated shoulder. He didn't dress or bandage any of my cuts. He didn't examine my leg. He didn't give me any pain medication, although I don't want the medication. I don't want to feel numb to the pain. The pain drives me.

All the doctor did was keep me alive.

And that's enough.

The drive to Milo's house seems almost as long as the plane ride. Getting jostled in the back seat of an SUV with a dislocated shoulder is the definition of hell, even with the makeshift sling I'm wearing.

But Enzo is safe.

That's what I keep reminding myself.

And soon the bastard in the front seat will be dead.

We get to the mansion and Milo walks ahead, while I follow. He doesn't tie me up or force me to follow. He just knows I will.

Then Milo leads me downstairs, and I panic. I want to stay in the light. I don't want to hide in the darkness.

But I follow because I need him to trust me. I need him to bring me into his world so I can take down his walls and stab his heart.

I don't know what Milo is going to do. *Is he going to hurt me now?* I know he is a patient man, in a similar way Enzo is. They must have both gotten that trait from their father.

I know Milo is concerned Enzo will attack him. And that might be the only thing that saves me.

We reach the darkness of the basement, and then I see the cage. A cage much nicer than any cage I've ever been locked in.

"Go," Milo says.

I skirt past Milo, but he grabs my hand at the last second before I can get inside the cage that will protect me from him.

He jerks me to his body, and I wince as my dislocated shoulder bumps into his chest.

"Don't think you are safe. Not for a second. I know your boyfriend will try to make a move. I need to focus on him for now. But soon, you will wish you hadn't made your deal. When I'm finished with you, your heart will no longer be Enzo's."

"My heart will always belong to Enzo."

His mouth crashes down on mine. I keep my lips closed, refusing to let his slimy tongue inside, but he grabs my chin and forcing my jaw open to push inside.

I squirm, my heart thumps quicker than a humming-bird's wings, my body trembles, and my breathing stops. I can't handle the invasion of his tongue in my mouth. *What if he tries more before I can stop him?* I won't survive.

He stops the kiss and looks me in the eye.

"I will steal your heart. You won't give it willingly, but before our time is over, it will belong to me. Not because you love me, but because you can't handle giving it away to any other man who will hurt you again."

I gasp, and he pushes me forcefully into my cage. He locks the door carefully and then walks up the stairs without another word.

As soon as he leaves, I break. I pant heavily as tears burn and my heart speeds.

I gasp, trying to catch my breath as I hunch over. Nothing has ever affected me quite like that. That kiss was the worst torture. That threat was the worst threat.

I reach into the sock of my boot and find the knife that

now seems stupid. It won't be enough against Milo. I need more. More to protect myself.

I consider pressing the earrings to alert Liesel to send in whatever men are stationed here. I can't wait for the perfect opportunity. But they would be sending the men to their deaths.

Milo is ready and waiting for Enzo to attack. We need to work down his patience. We need to get him vulnerable first.

I can do this.

I can save Enzo.

I pace around the room, trying to get the images that immediately flooded my head after that kiss out. But I know they are always going to be there hauntingly my dreams and even my thoughts. Of what that kiss threatened.

Milo will try to take everything from me.

He will try to rape me. But more than that. He will try to take away the love I have for Enzo.

I won't let him do either.

He doesn't get me as anything other than his prisoner.

I take long, deep breaths and finally feel the panic attack easing.

I sit down on the edge of the small mattress on the floor, careful not to hurt my arm.

When I close my eyes, I can feel Enzo. Milo kept him in this same room. I can smell his scent, see ruminants of his blood. And I pretend like the last time I was kept in a cage that Enzo is just on the other side of the wall, waiting for me.

I take another deep breath, and then I open my eyes— feeling better.

I examine my surroundings and try to figure out if there

is anything hidden in here that can help me, but I don't see much other than concrete, a water hose, and the bed.

I run my hand along the concrete wall behind me, and then I feel something poke me.

I turn to face the wall and find the small crevice. I dig at it and out falls something small and wooden.

I pick it up carefully and gasp as the tears start in again.

It's a tiny wooden heart with a small string at the top. I put it in the palm of my hand, and I know Enzo carved it.

There is an etching on it: *It's yours.*

His heart is mine.

Just like mine is his.

It's the closest thing to telling me I love you he's said.

Did he know someday I would end up in this cage same as him?

Or was this never meant to be passed on to me? Just something he carved for himself to be closer to me?

It doesn't matter because I've never been so thankful for a gift before. I study it more and find on the back he carved a K and an E.

I untie my hair with the scrunchie Zeke gave me and tie the heart to it like a charm added to a bracelet. The task is difficult with my dislocated shoulder, the task is worth the pain.

I have a piece of two of the men who matter most to me I can carry with me everywhere.

I tie my hair back up as best as I can with an injured arm in a sling and then touch the heart. "I love you too, Enzo."

And then I let my hand fall back to the small hole in the wall. And I know what I will find. Enzo needed a sharp knife to carve such intricate details of the heart.

I find the knife. I have two knives—two chances to kill Milo.

I leave the knife hidden where it is. If Milo takes the one in my sock, I have a backup.

But Enzo had access to a knife and never used it. *Why?*

Did he think it was the best way to keep me safe?

Or did he truly think it would start a war we might not win?

I know Enzo has faith in his men. I know he won't put them at risk unless absolutely necessary. That he wants to fight his own battles. But he needs to learn everything is personal in this business. And his men want to fight for him. Because they believe in him. They trust him. They will go to war for him.

"And who are you?" a voice startles me.

I turn around and see a charming looking man leaning against the wall across from the bars on my cage.

He's dressed casually in jeans and a buttoned-down shirt with the sleeves rolled up. The top couple of buttons are open, revealing a muscular chest with just a hint of dark chest hair.

"The better question is, who are you?" I ask.

He grins. "Ah, you haven't earned that yet. You haven't answered my question."

"I'm Kai."

His eyes open wide. "You're Enzo's girl."

I nod.

"Is Enzo… is he alive?" the tone of his voice changes as if he's concerned about him.

"It's not your turn to ask a question. I answered yours, now you answer mine. Then I will answer more. That's how this works. Give and take."

He grins. "I like you. My name is Felix. I'm a guard here."

"Yes, Enzo is alive." I refuse to say he *might* be alive. Or he was alive before I left, but he might be dead now. I have to believe he is alive.

"Good, Enzo and I became something like friends while he was here."

"Friends? I don't see Enzo getting friendly with one of Milo's guards."

He shrugs. "Believe what you want. But I don't always think Milo's way is the right way, especially with how he treats women."

His eyes heat as he speaks, and I can't tell if it's because he's angered by what Milo does or turned on. He's a hard man for me to read.

"But if you are here, then what happened to Enzo? He would never let you come here. He would defend you with his life, so he must be dead."

"I made a deal of my own. To save him."

He nods slowly before walking to the bars of my cage. He leans against them to get a closer look at me.

"You are tougher than you look."

"Why do you say that?"

"Because it looks like you've been in a car accident, then thrown from a high building, before being beaten up by twenty men. And you haven't once winced, moaned, or complained about how much pain you are in."

"Then I would say I'm just as tough as I look."

He looks to my shoulder. "Let me fix your shoulder. I can't do much about your leg, but I can fix your arm."

I nod.

I don't know if I should trust this man or not, but I don't have much of a choice. It would help a lot if my shoulder were back in place.

Felix unlocks the door and then steps inside my cage.

He doesn't bother to shut it or lock it back. He's trying to show me I should trust him. That he might be on my side.

But I don't trust easily. He earned Enzo's trust, and for now, that's all I know.

"Stand up and turn around," he says.

I do as he says, hoping he won't slice my neck or try to rape me.

"Close your eyes and picture yourself somewhere else. And bite down on something. This is going to hurt."

I laugh. "Do you know how much torture I've survived? I've had my shoulder dislocated and put back into place before. I can handle the pain without closing my eyes or imagining something else."

"I warned you."

He touches my arm, and I flinch.

"Told you," he smirks.

"It's not the pain from my shoulder. It's from your touch. I don't like being touched by strangers." I don't know why I told him that. It makes me vulnerable, but it's not something I can hide well.

"Sure, it is."

Ugh, he doesn't believe me. Well, I don't trust him. And my arm is tingling, sending alerts all through my body. There is something off about him, but I can't figure out what. I don't get the same feeling I do when Milo touches me, but it's not as calming as when Langston or even Liesel touches me.

"Ready?" he asks.

I nod.

And with a few twists and a pop, my shoulder is back in place.

He releases me, and I turn to stare at him.

"Thank you," I say.

He frowns. "You weren't kidding. The pain doesn't affect you."

I shrug. "When you've been through what I have, the pain is just different. It's part of my life."

He grabs my wrist again and watches my face twist from the touch. Then immediately lets go.

"I'm sorry. I believe you. I won't question you again," he says.

I nod. "Thank you again for fixing my shoulder." I test it a few times. It's very sore, but it's functioning normally again. In a few days, the pain will be a distant memory.

"I should go. I'll be back to check on you when I can. I really am Enzo's friend. You can trust me. If there is anything you need, I'm your man," he says before walking out.

I nod when he looks back. But I'm not sure I believe him. The vibes I get from him are so strange.

Maybe I just don't trust anyone anymore?

Enzo trusts him, so that's something. But I'd rather put my and Enzo's lives in my own hands if I can. Because trusting other people has gotten us both into trouble in the past.

20

ENZO

I WATCH the dot on the screen like it's my lifeline.

It is. It's my only link to Kai. And for the last twelve hours, it hasn't moved. Milo must have locked her away in the basement room I was locked in.

A room with all the basic necessities but not much more. But at least she'll have a bed to sleep in and water to drink.

Beyond that, I don't know what her current state is.

Is her shoulder still dislocated?

Is her leg still broken?

Is she bleeding from her cuts?

Is she barely clinging to life? Or did Milo pump her full of drugs, ensuring she stays alive?

I don't get answers to any of those questions. Instead, all I get is a little red dot on a map, showing that Kai is within the walls of Milo's compound—his impenetrable fortress.

The dot may be comforting, but the number showing her heart rate is what has me memorized. Sixty-three. Almost like clockwork, her heart beats at the same rhythm —sixty-three beats per minute.

I watch the blinking heart around the number representing every time her heart beats.

Blink.

Blink.

Blink.

Blink.

I hold my hand over my own heart, begging it to beat at the same speed. I need that connection right now. *God, how I need her.*

"Mr. Enzo," a meek voice says from behind where I sit staring at the laptop.

I take a deep breath, so I don't kill the young girl. I speak, but my voice still comes out deep and gnarly, "Yes, Yolie?"

"Kai is going to be okay. She's the strongest woman I've met. No matter what happens in there, she's going to make it," Yolie says.

I don't know if that shit is meant to comfort me or what, but I don't want to hear 'no matter what happens.' Nothing is going to happen. I won't let it. Kai is mine. *Mine, mine, mine.*

No man touches her.

"Yolie dear, why don't you come with me? I think Langston could use another run down of how Milo's security system works and how to override it," Liesel says, putting her hand on Yolie's shoulder.

"Sure, I'd love to explain it to him again," Yolie says cheerily, before running out of the room in the small cottage we found in Italy close to Milo's mansion.

"Langston is going to kill you for that," I say to Liesel.

Liesel smiles wryly. "Good, he deserves it."

I sigh. Liesel and Langston have always wanted to kill each other. Since we were kids, before life got so fucking complicated. And it seems to get worse with every year that passes. Zeke couldn't stand Liesel either. I'm the only one who has seen that beneath her hard exterior, which often comes across as bitchy, is a broken woman with one of the purest hearts I've ever seen. But Liesel doesn't let that side out often; you have to work to find it. And Langston definitely will take no part in spending enough time with her to find the good.

"You really fucked up, Enzo," Liesel says, stretching her legs up on the small coffee table as she leans back in the couch.

I want to keep staring at the dot and heart rate on my screen. I want to stare incessantly at the screen waiting for Kai to send a message that she is ready to be rescued. But apparently Liesel needs to talk to me, and it's not healthy for me to stare at a computer screen for twenty-four-hours a day.

"Yes, I know. But how specifically did I fuck up this time?"

"By making Milo's child, your heir."

I sigh. "We've been through this already." I run my hand through my unkempt hair. I could really use a haircut.

"Well, we are going to go through it again, because you are a fucking idiot, and you still don't have a solution."

"Does it matter if we kill Milo before he produces a child?" I ask.

"No, but what if he's already knocked a woman up and is holding her hostage in his basement? What then? If we kill Milo, his child will still become the next leader unless you are willing to kill a child," she says.

"I'm not."

"Then what is your genius plan?"

"I don't care about who leads my empire. I just want Kai safe."

"You don't get it, do you?" Liesel stands abruptly, with that look on her face that says she's going to win this fight. Except I don't even understand the rules.

She grabs me by the collar of my shirt, and jerks me up from my chair, yanking me toward the door.

"Jesus, woman. Calm down, I'm coming," I say, as I try to reach for the laptop.

"No, you don't get to bring that. Not everything is about Kai."

I growl.

She snaps back and pulls harder as she drags me out of the room. I could fight back, but I don't feel it's worth the fight. An angry Liesel would destroy this tiny cottage we are staying at, and we don't need to draw any attention to ourselves.

Liesel stops abruptly, and I slam into her back. "You could warn me when we are stopping," I say, but then my eyes cut around the room.

The cottage has a tiny living room connected to an eat-in kitchen and table for three. But this room currently includes a hundred of my best men and women.

"This is why you need a better plan," Liesel says, indicating to all the men and woman gathered ready to fight on my behalf.

"We put out a message that you needed help to get back the woman you love."

I try to say I don't love her, but Liesel doesn't give me room to talk.

"We said the mission was dangerous, personal, and voluntary. That no one had to participate. That you would never ask for their help in something so personal. This is just a fraction of the people who answered. These people believe in you. They believe you are good and worthy of leading them. They love their jobs, and they protect their families fiercely. This is your family. You can't just abandon them to a psycho. Most of them wouldn't follow him. They would either end up dead fighting against him or lose the only job they've ever known."

I swallow hard as I stare at all the people who believe in me.

"Sir," one of the women stands up. "You may not remember me, but you saved me from a terrible situation. I was sold, and you found me and brought me back to my family. You paid for my therapy. And then when I couldn't find other employment, you gave me a job at your club. I've shared my story, and most people in this room know someone you've helped, if not them personally. Thank you."

A man stands up. "Most of the men in this room worked for your father. We didn't care who he was because he paid well, and we all enjoyed using our weapons. We were fucked up and needed an outlet, and that was shooting and killing people. But your father was cruel and didn't give us second chances if we fucked up. He was a hard man to work for. And the reason we all kept working was you. We saw you at the club growing up. We saw the goodness in you from a young age. You weren't a saint, and you never will be, but you care about people. You protect people that need it. And we knew you would become a great leader when you finally took over."

"Thank you," I croak out, trying to keep my emotions in.

"And we are all bloody pissed about what Milo did to Surrender. That was our home he came in and destroyed. We want revenge."

I nod solemnly. To me, Surrender was a nightmare filled

with memories of my father, but to them, it was their home. Their place of work, where they came to relax, and where they were safe.

Liesel grabs my arm and pulls me away before I have a meltdown and cry in front of all these people who depend on me. She raises her eyebrow at me.

"You do have a heart."

I glare at her.

She smirks back and touches the scruff on my cheek. I know she still loves me. She probably always will. But any feelings I had for her beyond being my friend who I should protect, have long disappeared.

"This can't be just a mission to save Kai. This has to be about everyone. About destroying Milo, their enemy. About ensuring you are the leader of the Black empire. And about finding an heir who can take over for you when you are gone."

I nod slowly as I stare into her eyes. Liesel is right. "I don't know how I can accomplish all that."

"Well, one—kill Milo. And two—find a new heir," she says, but there is a mix of sadness and desperation in her voice. "Even if that means creating a new heir."

"Kai can't have children, though."

She nods. "I know. And I'm truly heartbroken for her. She will never be able to become the leader. But she was never meant to be. You were born for this. Raised to be a fearless king. And a king always has to have an heir."

I shake my head. I don't want to hear this. I refuse to have children with anyone who isn't Kai. I must have other relatives somewhere who can have children and become my heirs. Or I can find a loophole in the rules. Kai may not be able to lead, but I can. I just have to win one more stupid game and find an heir who I can mold into a leader. Then all those people in the other room will be safe.

"Does it make me a horrible leader if I still want to put Kai's needs above theirs?" I ask.

Liesel puts both her arms around my neck. "No, it makes you human. And as much as you want to put Kai's needs first, I know you. You won't hurt those people to protect Kai. You will find a way to protect all of them."

I nod.

Langston comes into the small bedroom we've ducked inside of and sees Liesel's arms around me.

He frowns at us.

"Yes?" I ask, stepping back, so Liesel's hands fall to her side. If Langston thinks anything is happening between Liesel and me, he's crazy.

"I've gone over the security info Yolie provided and the information you told us about the guards. We have him outmanned, at least of what we can tell, but he still has the home advantage. We could barge in and get through the gates, but we would be exposed. We would lose a lot of our team. And I'm not sure we would win. As much as I don't want to say this, it would be better if Kai found a way to give us an opportunity. A way in that didn't expose us. A way to distract Milo and his men."

"So, we wait."

He nods solemnly. He doesn't want to wait to get Kai back either. When I get her back, I'm going to wring her neck, and her ass is going to be so red she won't be able to sit for a year for what she did. But I know why she did it. She knew I needed to be the one to lead my team. The only way we would be able to defeat Milo was with the help of my army. And they would only follow me. She hasn't earned the title of king yet. In their eyes, I have.

"It would be helpful if you could figure out who his number two is. We need to know who is in line to take over Milo's position for when we kill Milo. We have to take out all of the leaders. Otherwise, even if Milo is gone, his number two could rebuild. He could gather our enemies against us, and we could still lose in the end."

"I know. But Milo was very tight-lipped about it. Even the guard I friended didn't know."

Langston leaves and returns with a pen and paper. "Write down every name you remember, even if you don't think they are in a leadership position. I will do as much research as I can on each name. And maybe if you write them down, it will become clearer. Maybe it will help you to connect a dot you didn't realize."

I don't know if it will help. But at least it will mean I'm doing something other than staring at a red dot all day.

I'm ready, Kai, just tell me when. Give me an opening, or give me a reason to put everyone at risk.

Everyone is ready to save her. To take down our enemy. And to take back our empire. But if I can't figure out who the number two is, will it be enough to save Kai and protect my team?

21

KAI

It's been three weeks.

Tortured doesn't even begin to describe how I feel. Not because I'm in any physical pain. In fact, I've never felt physically better as a prisoner before. But with each day that passes, my anxiety increases.

I long to be with Enzo.

But more importantly, I long for an ending. I want this to be over, whatever this is. I want to go head to head against Milo and determine a winner.

My arm rests in a sling and has almost completely healed. I try to force myself to do some exercises with it every day to strengthen it.

Felix brought me a splint for my leg, and it's helped take the pain off my shin. He's also brought me everything else I could possibly need—food, drink, books, even alcohol to help with my pain since he hasn't been able to find me any pain medications.

He's one of two guards on rotation to watch over me, and I look forward to when it's his turn on duty. He tells the best stories, listens to mine about Enzo, and ensures I'm taken care of. He's grown into a friend over the last couple of weeks.

I still get a weird feeling anytime he touches me, but I chalk it up to being trapped in this dungeon and not with him personally.

Felix is sitting in his chair outside of my cell reading a book, while I relax on the mattress on the floor reading Fifty Shades of Grey. Felix said all women like the book, and I do, but reading about Christian and Ana just reminds me of my own broken heart. It also makes me horny as hell and miss Enzo even more than I usually do.

Felix still has a few hours left in his shift, so I prepare myself to ask the same question I've asked him every day since I arrived. And I prepare myself for the same answer.

"Any chance you want to let me out of this cell for a few minutes? I could really use some sunshine and fresh air."

Felix smiles at me, knowing I was going to ask the question. I ask it every day.

It's not that I need the fresh air, although that would be nice. Three weeks in a dark room is nothing compared to the six years I spent in a cage.

The reason I ask is because I need to find a way for Enzo to get in. I need an excuse to explore. To see what Enzo saw when he was here. To find a way to distract Milo. I need a way for Enzo to get in.

"Tell me why you really want out, and maybe I will let you," he answers.

I flip the page of my book even though I haven't finished reading it. He knows. He knows why I want out. *And if I tell him the truth, will he let me? Or will he tell Milo my plan?*

I have to decide right now whether I trust him or not. Enzo trusted him, at least according to Felix he did.

But do I?

He's been nothing but kind to me. Brought me everything I have ever needed and more. He's talked to me like a
friend. And my gut has settled more around him each day.
But I don't fully trust him. There are only three men I
would trust to save me—Enzo, Zeke, and Langston. I don't
even fully trust Liesel. And I don't think I will ever let
anyone else into that small circle of trust. I guess having a
father who sold you will make you extra cautious.

So this isn't really about trust for me. It's not about
friendship either; I don't need to be his friend.

Can I use him?

The worst that will happen is he will tell Milo, but Milo
has already guessed Enzo is trying to figure out a way in to
save me. So it doesn't really matter if he finds out. And Felix
just might help me.

"I want out of here, so I can find Milo's weakness. I need
a way out of here, or more accurately, I need a way for
someone to get in undetected."

I wait.

And wait.

And wait.

Felix doesn't say anything right away. He just thinks
about what he's going to do with this information.

"Finally," he says.

"What?"

"Finally. I've been waiting for you to trust me for weeks.
I hate Milo. My brother died working for him. I hate how he
treats women. I want to bring him down. And I think you
and Enzo are the only ones capable of doing that."

Felix gets up and unlocks the door to my cage.

"Put your hand out," he says as he reaches into his back
pocket and produces handcuffs.

I frown.

"I'm sorry, but if anyone sees us, they need to see I still think of you as a prisoner and not a friend. These will help with that."

Reluctantly, I pull my arm out of the sling that has protected my shoulder all these weeks. It feels sore, but I stretch my shoulder and put my arms out.

Then Felix attaches the handcuffs to my wrists. He's careful to try and not touch my skin, but his fingertips brush my skin two times.

I wince both times as the stings zip through my body.

"Sorry," he says, noticing my reaction.

I smile weakly. "Don't apologize, you are helping me."

He shrugs. "Going to attempt to. Follow me."

Felix walks out of the cage, and when I reach the door, I stand hesitantly staring at the floor. He chuckles at my reaction, "Afraid of a taste of freedom?"

"No, it's just hard to be free when you've been captive for so long. It's hard to trust I can even do something as simple as walk out here, even though I have handcuffs and a guard."

He nods. "Trust me."

I nod. *I'll trust you as much as I can.*

I step out of the cell. I can do this. Milo isn't right around the corner, ready to jump on me. I'm going to be okay.

I follow Felix up the stairs slowly, my leg aching with each step. Finally, I reach the top, and Felix looks at me reluctantly.

"I need to hold onto you. If anyone spots us, it would look weird if I wasn't holding onto you or had a gun pointed at you. Your choice, I guess."

I would honestly prefer the gun, but a gun is riskier. A gun could accidentally go off.

I nod and look down at my injured right arm. I'm already used to feeling pain there. That's where he should touch me.

He gently grabs hold of my arm and then, without giving me time to think about it, leads me through the house.

I study everything as we walk, instead of focusing on the burning where he touches me.

We pass several servants but not too many guards. And the guards we do pass just give Felix a curt nod. They don't question what he's doing with me above ground.

We walk to the back of the house and don't spot Milo, but it doesn't stop my heart from racing. I try to keep my pulse as steady as I can, knowing the earrings will be sending my pulse rate to Enzo. And any increase will set him on edge.

Wait, Enzo, just a little longer. Give me more time to figure out a safe way in.

And then Felix stops and releases my arm, while he opens a bookshelf that leads to stairs.

"Here, here is your way in or out," Felix says.

I look down at the long staircase. "I want to go down."

I don't trust him at his word. It could be a trap; I need to know where it leads.

He just nods and holds the door for me to descend.

Slowly, I make my way down the stairs to what looks like a tunnel. "Does Milo know about this tunnel?"

"Yes, but he thinks he's the only one. He doesn't tell his security team because he doesn't trust anyone. He wants a way to escape if his team ever turns on him."

This is perfect.

We walk the entire tunnel. It leads up to a hidden entrance in a secluded garden near town.

When I feel the sun on me, I have the instinct to run. To get far away, but Milo would always be chasing us. And I'm not sure Felix would let me run anyway, it would be his ass on the line.

But I get to feel the sun for a few seconds. I try to memorize anything of importance that could help Enzo find the entrance. I notice a coffee shop across the street and take in the name. And then we make the long journey back to my cell.

Felix locks me back in my cell after removing my handcuffs. "How are you going to get the message to Enzo?"

I smile. He doesn't get to know that. "Don't worry about that. I'll make sure Enzo gets the information."

Felix reluctantly leaves me alone. And then I send all that I can through the earrings about the tunnel, where it starts, where it leads. I tell them to prepare. Soon, I will get them a distraction that will allow for them to enter.

Soon, this will all be over.

————

DAYS GET EASIER after Felix leads me to the tunnel. For once I have hope. Hope that my plan will work. Hope that Enzo will be able to save me. Hope that Enzo can become the leader he was destined to become. Hope that I will live long enough for him to love me back.

"You want some fresh air?" Felix says, stretching as he gets up from his chair. "Because I'm really tired of sitting in a dark basement all day."

I smile, loving the idea of being to go outside again. "Is it safe? Won't Milo find out?"

"No, he isn't here."

My grin shoots up to my eyes. "Let's go, then."

I jump up off the mattress on the floor and head to the door. Felix laughs at me, as I bounce anxiously behind the door like a dog about to be let outside for the first time in days.

He unlocks the door, and I stick out my wrists.

"What are you doing?" he asks.

"Waiting for you to handcuff me."

"No handcuffs."

I frown. "But what if Milo's men see us?"

"I'm one of Milo's men, remember? I'll just tell them I can easily overpower you, so I didn't see the need, which is the truth."

"Lead the way. I'm tired of this dark cell," I say.

Felix walks out of the dungeon and up to the main house. The light shining in immediately warms me. I never thought I'd be begging for sunlight. I much prefer the dark, but the light fits my hopeful mood. Today is the day I'm going to find a way to distract Milo. Today is the day I will send the information to Enzo. And then soon, we will put our plan into action.

The house seems empty, which is strange to me. The last time I was in the house, we ran into servants and guards. But this time, I don't see anyone.

"This way," Felix says, cocking his head to the right.

We walk down a long hallway, and Felix doesn't try to hold my arm once. We don't act like prisoner and guard. We act like two comfortable friends walking through the house.

Felix leads me out onto the back deck, and I gasp from the view.

"This is incredible," I say, walking closer to the edge of the deck, needing to get as close as possible to take in the most gorgeous landscape I've ever seen. Somehow this single view has everything—bright colored flowers, dark and light shaded trees, rolling hills, a streaming river, an overflowing waterfall, and mountains in the distance.

How could such an evil man live in such a beautiful place? How can the two worlds survive so close to each other?

"This is why I can't quit. This right here. Every day I consider quitting, and then I'm reminded I will have to give this up, and I stop," Felix says.

I stare at him, shocked at such an easy confession from him.

He shrugs. "The money Milo pays might also come into play. And the fact that if I quit, he'd probably have me shot."

I smile. "Don't let your job define your worth, Felix. Working for Milo doesn't make you evil. It's what's in your heart and how you try to use your power."

There is a pause, then, "Thank you, I needed that."

I look back at the view. "And I needed this. I needed a reminder; there is beauty in the darkest of places."

Felix's phone buzzes, and he pulls it out of his pocket.

"I need to take this. Don't run off," he says, stepping back inside, leaving me alone outside. But I know I'm not alone. There are cameras. There are guards. There are men all in this house who would be willing to hurt me if I took a step off this deck.

I take a deep breath of the fresh air trying to take everything in. There is so much to the world I have yet to see—so much good. Instead of experiencing it, I've been trapped in a world of torture and pain. This is what I want. A life where I seek out the beauty and bring light to those who can't see past the dark.

I decide to tap out a quick message for Enzo—*I'm safe. And this view is fucking incredible.*

When my hand drops, I feel more connected than I have since stepping foot here. My body is healing nicely. And

Enzo is ready to attack and has an undetectable entrance. I just need a way to keep Milo distracted long enough to not sound the alarm until Enzo has all the team in place. I don't know how many people will fight on our side, but I know it's more than Enzo thinks will come. More people believe in Enzo than just me.

I lean against the railing while I wait for Felix to return. I know I should only focus on one problem at a time. We need to kill Milo. He's too dangerous to us to stay alive. And then, when the dust settles, we can figure out how to finish the contract between our families to decide who should rule. We have one, possibly two more games to play. I would happily concede the games to Enzo, so he can win.

But the only way either of us can become the leader we have fought so hard to be is if we have an heir. If I kill Enzo's heir, then what do we have left? I can't have a child. And Enzo has no family left. He will have to have a child, and it can't be with me.

I hear the sliding door open behind me, but I don't turn around. Felix will talk to me when he's ready, and I want to enjoy my last few moments of peacefully staring out at the view.

A cold chill brushes through me, and I shiver. I don't shy away from the cold like most people; I welcome it in. But this is more than just cold wind rushing through me. It's more like a dark cloud descending over me, and bringing with it thunder, lightning, and a storm I won't be able to fight.

"Milo," I say, as the familiar chills of his presence pulses through me.

He doesn't answer; he simply steps forward to stand next to me.

I try to keep my body from reacting, but every cell in my

body responds to this man. He's physically hurt me. He's threatened the love of my life. He's tried to take an empire that isn't his to take. He's the worst kind of bully, the kind that needs you to bow down to him in order to feel powerful.

"When is Enzo coming for you?" his voice is gentle, light, not meant to be threatening, but intended to lull me into a false sense of calmness.

"He's not coming," I say as calmly back.

He snickers. "He's coming. He may not be capable of love like you are, stingray, but he can't let such a gem go, not without retaliation."

My head snaps to his. "What did you just call me?"

"Stingray."

"How...how do you know that name?" My bottom lip trembles as I speak.

"I won't answer your question, until you answer mine."

Lie, tell him what he wants to hear, make something up, because I have to know how he knows the nickname only three men have ever called me—the three men I trust more than anyone else in the world.

But I can't answer him, and he will refuse to answer me just to spite me.

"What do you want, Milo?" I ask, trying to let my curiosity go, and pretend he didn't just pull at my heartstrings by asking me that question.

His fingers brush over my shoulder blades, and my icy shield takes over, freezing him out. He won't be able to penetrate what is left of my heart. He won't be able to make me feel pain. I'm invincible.

And then he leans down to whisper in my ear, even though there is no reason to. There is no one here to hide his words from. But he does it because he knows how it will impact me, and he likes watching my body shutter.

"I always thought you were the stronger one. And I think in the end, you will be the one who wins."

I swallow, and I feel his eyes on my throat.

"Then why didn't you choose me to begin with? Why make a deal with Enzo if you think I'm going to be the one who wins?"

"More questions. What makes you think I will answer?"

"Because you want me to know the answers."

He smiles, smugly.

"So smart, my stingray."

"Is Zeke alive? Is he here? Are you torturing him?"

He chuckles. "You still believe in fairytales, don't you? You believe no one you love can truly die. Well, I'm sorry to be the one to break it to you, sweetheart. But people die. Every damn day. People who deserve to die and those that don't. It makes no difference. Everyone dies. And your friend, Zeke, is dead."

I step toward him with tears in my eyes. Not sure if I feel relief that Milo hasn't been torturing Zeke somewhere this entire time, or grief that Zeke is truly dead. He didn't make a miraculous resurrection like Milo did. He's just gone.

And maybe that's the least cruel thing of all. That Zeke doesn't have to live in this cruel world anymore. His soul is free.

"Then why did you call me stingray?" I ask. I see movement behind Milo—Felix. He's standing in the doorway watching us. I send him a look of help. To do something. To help me. Or to send for Enzo.

Felix disappears, and I have no idea if he's going to help me or not.

"If you want answers, then you answer me first," Milo's voice is dark and heavy.

I need to send for Enzo. I need to send out the alert, but my body is frozen with fear. From just the sound of his voice.

One long press and this can all be over. Enzo and his team will be running through the tunnels to get me. But I'm not ready. I shake off the frozenness of my body and realize I need an answer as badly as Milo needs an answer from me. The torturous wait will drive us both crazy.

So I answer Milo in the only way I can, "Enzo won't come until I call him."

I won't tell him how I can call him, but just that I'm the one who will make the decision. And then I wait for his answer.

"I got the information from your friend," he says, smiling as he says the word 'friend.'

My hand slinks up my neck, prepared to press the button on my earrings. I won't let Milo hurt me. It would kill Enzo as much as it kills me if he does. I just need to hear his answer first.

"What, friend?" *Surely, Langston or Liesel haven't been talking to Milo.*

"Felix."

Fuck!

My eyes go wide as I realize Felix has been telling Milo everything we have been talking about. I remember letting it slip that Enzo calls me stingray during one of our talks. Which means I can't trust the information Felix gave me. The tunnel is most likely a trap. I can't send Enzo to his death.

My hand falls away from my earring as I choose between my life and Enzo's. *It's not even a choice.*

Milo smiles. "You see, no matter what you do, you will lose. I'm smarter than you. I deserve the throne. I deserve to rule the underground not only here, but in America too. I will be unstoppable. I'll control the waters from here to Miami. But first, I'll make you my queen."

I laugh. "I will never be your queen."

"Maybe not, but you will have my child."

I cock my head. "No, I won't. I can't have children."

"Well, at least I will have fun trying."

I don't wait for him to speak again. I run. Enzo can't save me. I'm all alone. I run and run and run. I won't be taken. I won't let Milo have me. My plan failed. And if my feet fail, I will lose everything.

22

ENZO

KAI SENDS MESSAGES, but they aren't enough. I need more. I need daily, if not hourly, updates. I need to know more than broken messages. I need to hear her voice, see her face, hold her in my arms. Until then, the doom growing inside me is going to continue to increase.

Langston brings in a large sheet of paper, big enough to cover the bed.

"What are you doing?" I ask.

"You are going to draw a detailed map of the mansion, the guards you remember, the security, everything. We found the tunnels Kai told us about. We have the team ready to move in, but you are the only one that knows the layout of the inside."

I stare at the large, white piece of paper. I don't know if Langston is doing this because it will really help the men to know or if he's using it primarily as a distraction, but I take the marker from his hand and begin to draw everything I remember.

Liesel sits in the corner of the room watching me. She's

dressed in dark jeans and a tight T-shirt. She's staring at the gun in the back of my pants as I draw.

"You know you aren't coming," Langston says, as he looks at Liesel.

She frowns. "One—you don't tell me what to do. I don't take orders from anyone. Two—I can take care of myself. And three—I'm a part of this team same as everyone else. In fact, I came up with this plan, so I will be going if I want to."

"You aren't going," I say, without looking up.

"But—" she starts.

"You aren't going, Liesel, and that's final. You don't know how to fire a gun or have any combat skills. We don't need to worry about protecting you too. You will stay here with Yolie. You will be able to connect to the security system and alert us to where Milo's crew is," I say.

Liesel huffs but doesn't argue.

I continue drawing the map of everything I remember and try to distract myself from what Kai is going through.

But in a second, my world changes. The laptop makes a high-pitched sound, and we all run to it—Langston, Liesel, and me.

"What's happening?" Liesel asks.

"I don't know. An alarm is sounding. Did Kai send an alert to be rescued?" I ask, staring frustrated at the screen.

The door opens, and Yolie pops in.

She races to the laptop, pushing me out of the way to look at it.

"What's happening? Is Kai alerting us?" I ask.

"She hasn't pressed the button to send for us, but her heart rate is up. Dangerously up. Two-hundred and climbing."

"It could be from exercise. You said Felix took you out to exercise twice a day," Langston says, trying to calm us.

"He wouldn't do that for Kai. Milo wouldn't want her strong to be able to defeat me. He would want her weak. And she hasn't gotten to exercise in the weeks she's been there," I answer.

"People's heart rate goes up for a variety of reasons, it doesn't mean she's in distress," Liesel says.

But Yolie's look tells me she is on the same page as me. Kai's heart rate never goes up. She's calm, too calm sometimes. This isn't exercise. This isn't a nightmare she's dreaming about. This isn't simple distress at overhearing a conversation or anxiety from being trapped in a cage. This is different. This is life or death. Which means our time is up.

"What do you want to do?" Yolie asks.

"I want to go rescue the woman I love."

23

KAI

I RUN for an hour before my feet fail me.

Each step was painful. I haven't been wearing the sling around my arm and running that hard, and that fast through unstable terrain has left my shoulder throbbing.

My still-healing leg burned with every step, barely keeping up.

But worst of all was the worry in my chest. I tried to stay calm, knowing Enzo would notice the rise in my heartbeat, and any change would cause him to run to my aid.

So with each step, I kept my breathing slow. I focused on the beauty of the ground, instead of the heavy panting growing closer behind me. And my heartbeat held.

With every moment that passed, the urge to press my earring and alert Enzo to come grew stronger. I need his help. I won't survive without Enzo coming for me.

But we can't trust Felix. It could be a trap.

I considered trying to type out a message as I run, but that would have slow me down too much. Milo would have caught me.

I'm surprised he didn't catch me quickly. But then again, Milo probably liked the chase.

But then my broken shin hit a rock. I didn't lift my leg high enough to step over it. And I tumbled down to the ground.

Now I lay eyes closed on the hard earth with Milo standing over me.

I just lost the biggest battle of my life.

I can feel the darkness consuming me already. He's only standing near me, but my brain is working overtime imagining all the things he will do to me. All the ways he will break me. All the ways he will ruin me.

Press the button. Tell Enzo. Come save me.

But I would never want Enzo to risk his life to save mine. *I love you, Enzo.* Hopefully, my love for you will get you through the pain that will await you when you do finally find me.

I open my eyes when I'm ready to face the darkness.

Milo has crouched down and is staring at my face.

"I once loved as you do. But that love was taken from me in the worst possible way. Because of that, I no longer have a heart. And I make it my mission to destroy anyone else who I see loves like I used to. You shouldn't love as strongly as you do. Love shouldn't consume you. It will take everything from you."

I feel his pain with every word. He was hurt in a way I have yet to experience, but I'm afraid Milo is about to show me.

Milo grabs my neck before I have a chance to move.

And then he pushes my legs wide apart as he settles between them.

Shut down, now. Shut down! I scream at my body. *I can't feel this. I'll never survive.*

Milo's eyes turn sad. As if what he's going to do will break him as much as it will break me. "You don't deserve this. If I could do this to Enzo, I would. He's the one who deserves this. But I have to teach one of you a lesson. It's the only way you will learn how wrong loving someone else is."

"Please, just let me go. Don't rape me," I whisper.

Milo shakes his head.

"My body will only open the hole in your heart to get you to listen to me. My story is what will cause you to give me your heart willingly."

I have no idea how those words can be true, but in the end, I'm afraid they just might be.

24

ENZO

THE TUNNELS WORK LIKE A CHARM.

We get into the mansion completely undetected. And Felix is waiting for us when we reach the end.

"I've already switched the cameras to your feed. No one knows you are here," Felix says.

"Thank you," I say, happy Kai learned to trust Felix in the same way I did. "We have teams at all the gates ready to break them down, and my team is filing up through the tunnels quickly. We are bringing this entire organization down."

Felix nods. "Good, this needs to end."

"It does."

"Where is Kai? Milo?" I ask.

"Not sure, watch out," Felix says, firing his gun behind me.

And so the war starts.

I start shooting, and Langston follows up behind me. It feels weird not to have Zeke on the other side watching my other shoulder. We are incomplete with just the two of us, and it's all the more reason to make Milo and his entire team suffer—for Zeke.

I don't think as I take down man after man. My brain switches to automatic fighting mode, and that doesn't include any emotions. I could probably single-handedly take down every man in this mansion. My father programmed me that way. But there are more of Milo's men outside the mansion, more gathering nearby. And I have hundreds of people ready to fight them all for me. Because they want me to be their leader.

I see the blood of my enemies being spilled, and the sight only drives me further deeper into the house.

"Any sign of Milo or Kai?" I ask into my earpiece.

"No, we don't see either of them on any of the security cameras," Liesel answers.

I growl. Either Milo knew I was coming and turned the ones aimed at him off, or they are somewhere the cameras aren't.

The basement.

They must be there. "How is her heart rate?" I ask as I fire another shot.

Silence.

Fuck, fuck, fuck.

"Kai is strong, just stay alive," Liesel says.

I can't stay alive if Kai is hurting.

I fire off several rounds, pushing men back as I make my way to the stairs. I have to find her. I need to know she is safe.

I reach the basement stairs being guarded by five men. My suspicions were correct; they are in the basement.

One, two, three, four, five.

That's how long it takes me to take down five men with five shots.

They all fall, one blocks the door with his limp body, but I pull his corpse away from the door as easily as I would move a sack of potatoes.

I throw the door open, practically yanking it from its hinges, and then I run down the stairs with my gun aimed. If I see Milo touching Kai, I will kill him without giving him one more second to breathe.

Down into the hole underground I go.

"Kai!" I scream into the darkness, but I see nothing. I get no answer.

"Kai!" I yell again.

I run to the cage Milo kept me in. The door is open, and I dart inside even though I can clearly see through the bars the room is empty.

Kai was here. I can smell and feel her in every essence of the room. I don't see any blood, no sign of a struggle. Whenever she left, she left willingly.

I walk over slowly to the bed and feel in the crevices of the wall. The heart I carved is gone, but the knife remains.

Fuck, she has no weapon.

But she took the heart. When I started carving it, I didn't think she would ever see it, it was for me. But I think somewhere in my heart, I knew she would be here, and she would need it.

Please let it be enough to protect her. She still hasn't pressed the alarm on her earrings. *Please be somewhere safe. Please know that I love you.*

"Enzo!" Langston yells.

I look up with a gloominess in my eyes.

"Have you found her?" I ask.

"No."

A deep fear grows stronger in my belly. *Where are you, stingray?*

"But the mansion is secure. The grounds are secure. We won," Langston says.

"No, we didn't win until we find Milo and Kai. Not until Milo is dead, and Kai is safe. That's when we win."

"Have you found her?" I say into the earpiece.

"No," Liesel answers.

"I thought the earrings were supposed to be able to track her."

"They are, but wherever she is, we lost the signal," Liesel says.

Fuck.

Langston nods. "What is our next move?"

"Are there survivors?" I ask, meaning our enemies.

"Yes."

"Bring me them. And Felix. I want answers," I say.

Langston heads upstairs and brings me two of Milo's guards.

"Felix?" I ask Langston.

He shakes his head as he shoves one of the men toward me. The prisoner's hands are tied with rope.

I pull a knife from my pocket. "Tell me where Milo and Kai are."

I'll do whatever it takes to get answers. Every second that passes is another where Kai could be in incredible pain. Each second that passes is one where I might never get her back. And these two men will be the first to understand just how far I will go to find her.

25

KAI

IT'S BEEN HOURS. *Or has it been days or years?*

Reality doesn't exist for me in the same way anymore. All I know is darkness covers the sky.

Milo's body is on top of me. He's in me. He's around me. He's everything I am.

I don't fight anymore.

I gave up fighting within the first hour.

And since then, everything has changed.

Pain is different than it was before. It's stronger somehow, yet foggy at the same time. But I no longer fear pain. It is who I am now. I am pain. And agony. And despair. That's where I exist now.

But Milo was right. The physical pain just opened the hole to my heart; his words finished me.

Milo is Enzo's younger half-brother.

Enzo's father is Milo's father.

I thought Enzo experienced pain at his father's hand, but his experience was nothing compared to Milo's. When Milo told me his story, I cried for him. *How fucked up is that?*

I felt pain for the man who raped and destroyed me.

God, my mind is so foggy. Am I remembering right? Did I really cry for Milo? I couldn't have.

Milo said so many things.

So many truths spilled from his lips. He's a monster, but he's also a broken boy who has lost the love of his life.

It doesn't absolve him of his sins, but it helps me to understand him. He's as human as Enzo or I am. He's experienced pain in a similar way we have, but the difference between him and us, is what he did with that pain.

We turned our pain into love.

He turned his pain into anger.

And that level of anger becomes so dark and evil, there is no coming back from it.

I don't feel, but not because I've turned everything off. Not because I've put up my icy shield and gone numb like I have hundreds of times before.

I don't feel because I gave Milo my heart and my love. That's not to say I love Milo—I don't. But I willingly surrendered my heart to him.

Words are strong, the most powerful tool any of us have. And Milo is an expert storyteller. The way he spoke was a weapon against my heart and love for Enzo.

And in the time we spent together, Milo obliterated any love I could ever hope of having.

That's why I will never experience emotions again. Milo stole them, and I don't ever want them back.

My eyes look deep into Milo's. That's why he's able to hurt me like he is, because he has no heart either.

Milo shouldn't have done what he did to me. He had no right. But the words he spoke needed to be said.

Yet that doesn't stop what I need to do next.

My surroundings slowly come back into view after hours of darkness. The soft, wetness of the grass we are laying on. Milo's cold body on my nakedness. The trees surrounding us, making it impossible for anyone to find us.

I suck in a breath, but it's not enough, Milo's weight is too much for me to get a good breath. *Why is it that even though my heart is gone, I can still feel all the pain?*

And this pain of Milo ripping and forcing himself inside my body will never end if I don't stop it. Enzo will never find me here in the middle of the woods. We could be here days more before he finds us. *I have to end this.*

Tears wet my eyes again as I come back to reality. Of how many times I was raped. Of how my life changed in a few hours.

But I have to take back control.

I look around for anything I can use to try to get Milo off of me. I tried before he started. But my body was weak compared to his.

I tried reaching for the knife around my ankle, but I couldn't reach it.

I even got desperate enough to press the button on my earrings, but Milo grabbed my arms, and I haven't been able to move them freely again, until now.

Milo looks as exhausted and tormented as I am.

But that doesn't stop him.

Nothing will.

Until I end this.

I go through the same motions as before, this time, more delirious. I search for rocks to slam into his head. But all I see are weak looking sticks.

My earrings! I can press my earrings. I squeeze the button on them tightly, trying to alert Enzo to where I am. But my hope quickly diminishes. Even if he finds me, the damage has already been done.

And then I see my clothes—bloodied and ripped,

discarded next to me.

Milo continues his movements, pumping, but not really putting his whole heart into it anymore. While I search for my knife.

Please, please, please.

Shirt.

Pants.

Shoe.

Sock!

And tucked beneath the sock, is a thin blade of a knife.

Milo's eyes are closed as he rocks.

Slowly, I reach out and grab the knife.

And then I do what I must—what has to happen for this to end. Even though I know the consequences of what I'm about to do. Milo may be bad, but his successor will be worse.

I grip the knife with both hands and use all of my force to stab into his chest, aiming for his heart.

I pull back, watching the blood squirt. And then I stab *again, again, again, again, again, again, again...*

So much pain, anger, and anguish go into each stab.

Die, die, die, die.

I hate you.

I hate your truths.

I hate it all.

I pant heavily, tears falling freely, blinding my vision as I stab. *Over and over.*

And over and over.

And over and over.

Everything consumes me in that moment.

"Stingray..."

The single word brings me out of the fog.

And I weep.

26

ENZO

MILO IS DEAD, and Kai is alive.

I repeat the words over and over in my head, trying to erase everything else I see from my brain.

But I can't.

I'm so tortured.

And this moment will change me. I'm not sure how yet. But it will. Just like it changed Kai.

I walk slowly to her even though I want to run. I need to keep her calm and get her out of here without her seeing anything else.

Langston is standing behind me, and I hold up a hand for him to wait. I don't want to overwhelm her, and I don't know what her current state is.

"Stingray," I say softly again.

Her watered eyes stare at me, but thank god, the bluish-green color is still there. There is still life behind her eyes, even if she doesn't feel it yet.

"Can I have the knife?" I ask. I'm afraid if I touch her, she will start stabbing at me. And while I could easily block her, I don't want her to have any guilt later for attempting to hurt me.

She drops the knife, and I toss it away.

"I need you to close your eyes for a second, stingray," my voice is sweet sounding and calm. My breath is flowing and light like a feather. And I hope it's enough for her to listen to me.

I see the determination in her eyes. She wants to keep her eyes open, now that she's found something to hold onto. But she can't. She needs to close them so I can get rid of Milo.

I'm not even sure she realizes he's dead yet.

Slowly, she closes her eyes.

And then I ease Milo's body off of her. She winces when he's free of her.

All I see is blood.

Hers.

His.

It all mixes together covering both of their naked bodies.

This image will haunt me forever.

I failed.

Again.

And I don't know if our relationship will ever recover from this—from me failing her. From the pain she endured. I don't know if even time can heal this.

I quickly remove my shirt.

"Stingray, can I put a shirt on you?"

She nods and sits up, putting her arms up over her head.

Whatever is going on inside her head, at least she can hear me. She still trusts me enough to help her.

I carefully slip the shirt over her body, even though I

want to wipe her clean of the blood first. I don't touch her skin, as much as I want to. I won't be selfish, not with her.

I won't hurt her.

"Keep your eyes closed for a few more seconds," I tell her.

She nods.

And then I wave to Langston.

We both stand over Milo's lifeless, mutilated body.

"Jesus," Langston curses as he looks from Kai to Milo. "What do you want me to do?"

"Bury his body. And then take care of the team and Liesel. I need to..." But I don't know what to do. I just know Kai needs me.

Langston nods as he goes to Milo and grabs his feet. He begins dragging him through the woods.

And as much as Milo got what he deserved, I have a strange sense of loss at seeing him go. Something I can't explain. But I won't focus on it. I have someone more important to focus on.

I kneel in front of Kai. "Okay, you can open your eyes."

Her eyes blink open as soon as I speak.

I bite my lip.

She notices. But she doesn't touch me. She doesn't kiss me. She doesn't throw herself into my arms now that she is free.

"We need to get out of here," I say.

She nods.

"Can I carry you?"

She nods.

And I'm afraid that may be all I ever get again from her —a nod.

I lift her body, and it feels different than any other time I've touched her. The spark is gone. But then again, that is to be expected. She was just raped. And I just went through a war to find her.

But we've been through bad times before, and every time, the spark was there.

Every time but this time.

And a little more of my hope leaves me.

I carry her through the woods to my waiting car. Langston and I drove here together when the signal finally came through from her earring. It was no longer sending out a signal of her location unless she pressed the button, which she finally did, but only after it was too late to save her.

Langston will have to find his own way back.

I consider putting her in the backseat. But it's too far away from me. The seat next to me is too.

So I push the driver's seat back as far as I can, and then I sit down with her in my lap. It's not comfortable for either of us, but she doesn't complain or ask for me to move her.

Probably because she isn't speaking to me again. This will be just like before. *Maybe worse.*

I start driving, taking her away from the destruction of our world. And hoping to find something that resembles healing in the horizon.

I should drive back to the cottage we rented, but I don't. I can't deal with people right now. Kai can't either.

So I drive toward the water.

Some of our men brought one of the yachts over. But it's empty because everyone was focused on killing Milo and his men.

I park the car on the side of the road and carry her up to the yacht. The water has been the thing that has brought us together and torn us apart more than anything else. *Maybe it can do it one more time?*

If nothing else, it will give us a place to be alone for a while. Because completely alone might be the only way we will heal.

I holler for a dockhand to untie us. And then I head to the helm and start the engines with Kai still in my lap.

We head out into the darkness of the night. But the darkness never bothered us. Until now...

———

I DID everything I was supposed to do.

I made sure she bathed and put on clean clothes.

I got her food and water.

I never left her alone.

But now, I have no idea what to do.

Do I try to get her to sleep?

Do I try talking?

Do I leave her alone?

Do we sit on the deck and breathe in the fresh air?

Do I kiss her?

Do I hug her?

What do I do?

We've been here before, in the depths of a darkness I never thought we'd dig ourselves out of. And we survived. But this time, it feels so different.

"I will do anything for you. Just tell me what to do," I say.

She nods.

"Or maybe, write it down," I jump up from where we are sitting on the top deck staring out into the starry night and dark blue sea below.

She grabs my wrist, stopping me from leaving.

There it is.

I sigh in relief.

The spark is back. It's weak, so fucking weak, but I feel its trembles stirring in my body.

"I'll stay," I say, sitting back down next to her.

She continues to grip my wrist.

Maybe this is what I do. Just sit here with her. Until she's ready.

"Fuck me, Enzo."

My ears must not be working. I didn't expect her to say that.

"I'm sorry, I think I misheard you."

"No, you didn't."

I swallow down the shock as I stare into her eyes. I expect to see broken. I expect to see pain. I don't expect to see clarity.

"Why? I mean...um...are you sure that's what you really want right now? I can hold you. Or kiss you. Comfort you. We don't have to—"

"Fuck me, Enzo."

I will give her anything she wants, and there is nothing more I want to do than fuck her and remove any remnants of Milo from her body. But I'm not sure it's the right move for her.

"Stop thinking and fuck me." She kisses me, hard. Harder than all of our other kisses. And then, I'm no longer thinking. I just have this animalistic desire to be inside her.

And her kiss proves that's what she needs too.

I grab her neck harder than I meant to, pulling her body onto my lap.

She's wearing a T-shirt and baggy sweatpants I found in one of the cabins, while I'm wearing jeans and T-shirt. And I want all the clothes gone.

She moans into my lips, "Yes."

She's reading my mind and giving me permission to remove all her clothes.

Kai keeps kissing me hard on the lips, and I know both our lips will be bruised and bloodied in the morning from the intensity of the kisses. But neither of us care.

I grab the hem of her shirt and lift up, breaking our kiss to remove the shirt.

She doesn't give me a second to examine her body; her lips devour mine again. She moans against me, and I have the strongest desire ever to make her feel incredibly good.

My hands find her nipples, pointing at me, begging to be touched. I flick over them, and her body arches needing more.

"That feel good, baby?"

"Mmh," she purrs, unable to get any words out.

I grin into her lips. "I think you love it when I do this." I squeeze her nipples and watch her reaction.

She moans into my lips, grabbing my hair forcefully, and pulling my body to hers. Her thighs squeeze over mine, and my erection pushes up toward her.

"I want something else more though." I grab the waistband of her pants and lower them as much as I can. Then I move her off me, so her pants drop the floor, so she's naked in front of me.

"Even more beautiful than I remember."

But from the heat in her eyes, I know she's not here for my romantic comments.

I quickly lower the lounger back until I'm laying flat, and then I grab her waist. I don't want either of us to have time to think. If we do, then we will stop. And I want to give this a chance to heal us. To see if fucking each other is what we need to get back together.

I part her legs, and she sinks down onto my face.

And when I taste her sweet pussy, I don't think about anything other than pleasuring her.

My tongue takes its time finding her clit, first licking around her lips and teasing her slit.

Her body rides my face, moving in gyrating circles, trying to get my tongue to stop her agony.

She growls—making me laugh.

And I finally give her what her body craves.

My tongue on her clit.

I lick quickly, making up for lost time. And she grinds into my tongue, begging me to move it faster. So I do.

Faster, faster, faster.

I want to put a finger inside her, but she rides my lips so hard there is no room. And from the sounds she is making, I know she doesn't need my fingers to get off. *Just this, my mouth fucking her.*

"Come, stingray," I purr over her clit—the vibrations adding another layer of sensation for me before she explodes on my face.

"Yes!" she screams.

I smile up watching how beautiful she is as she comes. And how Milo may have taken so much, but he didn't take this.

It takes her a while to come down from her high, but slowly, she looks at me and says, "More."

I know what more means—*fuck her.*

I nod—now I'm the mute one.

She scoots her body down, pulling at the buttons of my jeans. She slowly undoes them and pushes my pants down, wiggling them off my body.

She rests over my hips, and I hold her gently, giving her space to fuck me when she's ready. But her eyes tell me this isn't what she wants.

"What do you want?" I croak.

"For you to fuck me."

I nod. She doesn't want to be on top.

Carefully, I roll us around on the lounger until she is underneath me.

I've never been so scared in my life. My body is hard as steel, that won't be the problem. But I'm scared that with one thrust I could ruin everything we've gained.

I want to tell her I love her. But a few hours after the worst night of her life doesn't seem like the right time. So I don't. When I tell her, I want it to be the only thing on either of our minds.

Slowly, I spread her legs and watch her breathing speed.

"We don't have to, stingray."

"Stop calling me stingray."

I sigh. "I'll do whatever you want, baby. Just tell me what you want." It hurts she doesn't want me to call her stingray. She may think Zeke was the only one that had any input in that name. He may have taken credit for it and told her first, but it was as much mine as his. It was as much Langston's as his. It's the name three men who love her use to describe her. And it hurts she doesn't love the name anymore.

But if she doesn't want me to say the name tonight, I won't.

"Fuck me," she says again, grabbing my hips to pull toward her.

My cock rests between her legs, but I'm not sure I can enter her without her push. I don't want to hurt her after what she went through.

She reaches up to my neck, and starts kissing me, and we both forget. We get lost in the kiss. I can't get close enough to her. Closer and closer our tongues slip inside. Our chests press together. And...

...then I'm inside her.

As if I've always belonged inside her. As if nothing has changed. It feels as spiritual as any other time I've fucked her. She is still my home.

I rock, and she moans in delight.

Kai is still mine.

Everything else disappears. And only us exist. This wonderful connection Kai and I share is back in full force. We just needed this connection of our bodies to find it again.

I fuck her slow.

I fuck her fast.

She fucks me back.

Time moves differently, but eventually, she comes, and then I do too, in a beautiful ending to the worst story of my life.

But when I pull out of her, everything changes. And I realize that wasn't a welcoming home. That was a goodbye.

I hold her in my arms, trying to get the feeling back, but it doesn't come. And as she closes her eyes and drifts off, I realize the darkness is still upon us. And that darkness is stronger than ever before.

27

___

KAI

Milo...

"No!"

"Stop!"

.

.

.

"Shut up, whore."

I shut up. It's easier if I'm quiet.

.

.

.

"Now, I'm going to tell you a story. About me and my brothers: my half brother, Enzo; my twin brother, Pietro; and my younger brother, Felix."

28

ENZO

"Kai has been like this for hours. I can't wake her up," I say to the doctor.

Langston and Liesel are standing behind me looking horrified as we all stare down at Kai, lying in the bed, clearly in torment. At first, I thought she was just having a nightmare, but then I couldn't wake her up.

I tried shaking, talking, yelling, tapping, sitting her up, pouring water over her, nothing worked.

The doctor ignores me and continues to check her over. He listens to her heart for a few more minutes, and then he looks at the three of us waiting for answers.

"Everyone deals with extreme situations differently. And this is how she is handling the trauma. When she was experiencing it, her brain must not have processed everything that was happening to her the first time. Something triggered the trauma, and she's processing it all now."

I triggered her, by fucking her.

I run my hand through my hair. "What can we do?"

He looks from me to her. "I can sedate her, which would

put her into a deeper sleep and get rid of the nightmares, but—"

"Do it," I say. *I need her pain to stop.*

"But this could keep happening over and over until her brain has processed what has happened to her. It may be better to just let her body run its course," the doctor continues.

"Sedate her," I say.

"Enzo, take a second and think about what Kai would want. She's never shied away from dealing with her pain. Maybe you should let her body do its thing. And when this is over, then she can work on healing in a healthy way," Liesel says.

"Fuck!" I yell, hoping somehow that it will wake Kai up, because I don't want to make the decision.

"Give her twenty-four-hours to rest in her own way. Process what happened as it comes. Then we can make a decision to either sedate her or wake her up. I've given her some pain medication, so either way, she won't be in physical pain," the doctor says, getting up.

Langston and Liesel thank him, but I just go and sit next to Kai.

Milo is gone. His empire is in shambles. And there is no threat of a successor to take his place. *Kai is safe.*

But I can't save her from her nightmares. And I can't protect her from her past.

"Tell me what to do, stingray. Tell me what to do."

29

KAI

In.

Out.

No, stop focusing on what he's doing.

.

.

.

I scream.

I cry.

I lose my mind, and Milo wants to tell me a fucking story while he rapes me. But maybe his words will be what will help me survive.

"My father didn't visit Felix, Pietro, or me often, but when he did, it shook us all to our core. We all knew he had another family. *His real family out there.* We were just his spares. The ones he kept hidden in case his first son wasn't strong enough to take over his empire."

More thrusts. *No focus on his words, not what he is doing.*

"Pietro was the oldest by two minutes, so father focused on grooming him the most. Father thought he would make a good replacement for Enzo, if Enzo were to fail. But that didn't mean Felix or I were off the hook. We all had to be ready. And he promised us our own, smaller empire he would help us build in Italy if Enzo were to succeed."

Milo's fingers claw at my hips too harshly, and I cry out. I thought I could shut him out, but it's impossible.

I'm not going to survive this.

.

.

.

The back of my head hits the ground now with every thrust. Tears still sting my eyes. And his story continues.

"One year, when we were thirteen, he came back. It was the last time. And he brought Enzo. I don't think he knew who we were, but we knew who he was. *The heir. The chosen one.* The only son our father truly loved."

.

.

.

This has to end!

My tears have stopped. And my muscles shiver with weakness and shock.

Please, stop.

"We soon realized why Enzo was here. Our father had a final test. One where Enzo could prove he was truly worthy of being his heir. Father handed him a gun. And said choose."

I gasp, my eyes flying to Milo's filled with pain.

"Pietro and I were the closest. We were twins. We did everything together."

Milo cries.

And my eyes drip for the boy. The boy whose father broke him. And the man I love who played his part.

"Enzo didn't even blink. He lifted the gun and shot Pietro. He was just a kid—just thirteen."

His brother was the love of his life. Not a woman. His brother—*Pietro*.

And for the tiniest of seconds, I understand Milo's pain. He didn't deserve that any more than I deserved to be taken and beaten or raped.

But my pain I turned into beauty, his pain he turned into rage. And he's never been able to escape it.

"Why? Why did you tell me?" I whisper, trying to forget where his cock is right now.

"So you know who the man you love really is. And so you believe me when I tell you the truth."

30

ENZO

I waited the fucking twenty-four hours, never leaving Kai's side.

It was the worst hell I've been through, watching her seemingly relive her nightmare. And all the time I was hoping I did the right thing. I hoped when she woke up, she would be able to start the journey toward healing.

I even broke my promise and told her I love her, but even that didn't wake her from her nightmare.

Finally, her nightmare stopped. She woke up. But Kai was gone.

She didn't speak.

She didn't look at me.

She didn't move.

She didn't eat.

She didn't breathe.

She didn't drink.

And sometimes when I look at her sitting there in her chair and looking out the yacht window to the ocean, I wish she were asleep again. Because asleep, I still had some hope. *But now I have none.*

It's been weeks. Over a month and nothing has changed.

She just sits.

Occasionally, she sleeps.

And Liesel is the only one who can get her to eat.

Otherwise, Kai ignores us all.

I've tried everything. The doctor says she just needs time, but I don't think Kai is even fighting anymore. I'm afraid Milo stole what makes Kai, Kai, and he took her with him to hell. And I'm left with the shell of her body.

But I won't stop trying. I will never give up on her. And I know the next round of games to become Black is nearing. Maybe that will wake her up. But I doubt she would even show up. And I have no idea if I can legally take over the company if I don't finish the games and have a child who can claim the throne after me.

I head into Kai's room. As usual, she is sitting alone, staring out the window.

I take a deep breath, trying to push my own selfish pain away. She doesn't need to feel my pain. She needs my help.

So I walk over to her and kneel in front of her as I do every day. I want to take her hand, but I hate forcing her to do anything. Although, I've broken that promise a few times over the month and a half now.

"I love you, Kai. You are the love of my life, come back to me..."

31

KAI

"Come back to me..." Enzo says.

It's the same words he says to me every single day.

But I can't come back.

I'm not the same person.

And Enzo isn't the person I thought he was. Milo reminded me how many people Enzo has killed. He may have saved many women, but he's killed more.

I blink, know that was just the conditioning. Milo wants me to hate Enzo. *Stop thinking that!* I scream at myself.

But I don't show Enzo any of the turmoil going on inside me. I'm not quiet because of the trauma of what Milo did to me; I'm quiet because I need the quiet to work through the chaos inside my head.

Enzo stays one hour before he can't be calm anymore. And then he leaves. A few minutes later, Liesel enters the room.

She never goes easy on me. Not like Enzo and Langston do. I haven't spoken to her, but I've heard everything on her mind.

How I need to woman up. How I need to put Enzo out of

his misery and just say something, anything. How I'm being a little bit selfish.

But she also says how sorry she is. She cries. She gets mad at Milo and curses him.

And then she smiles at me when she asks me how good it felt to kill him.

I may not answer back, but that doesn't stop Liesel. And our friendship grows in an unexpected way as she tells me all of her own truths.

About her and Enzo.

About Langston and their weird relationship.

About her apartment.

About how she secretly hates yachts, but don't tell Enzo that.

About how she wants to get a dog but thinks she is allergic.

About everything on her mind.

And with every truth she tells me, I want to tell her the one that changed me. The single truth that will change everything.

I smile, well two truths.

Liesel notices my smile. "You smiled!" she squeals.

I frown.

And she snaps her hand over her mouth. "Sorry, I shouldn't get Enzo's hopes up." She walks over to the door and closes and locks it before sitting in the chair next to me.

"There, now we are alone. Smile away. Don't worry, I won't brag to Enzo that I was the one who got you to smile." Liesel leans back in her chair.

And I know the only way I'm going to get this out.

"Truth or lie," I say, my voice breaking.

Liesel leans forward, her mouth drops, and she stares at me blinking, not understanding. But I can be patient. I've waited a month to tell anyone my truth. And I only have enough strength for a limited amount of words.

Finally, Liesel says, "You want to play truth or lies with me?"

I nod.

"Okay," Liesel says, waiting.

"I'm pregnant," I say.

Liesel gasps and stares at my stomach like I'm already showing. *I'm not. It's only been a month.*

"Truth or lie?" I ask.

"Oh, right, the game. Truth—you're pregnant," Liesel answers.

I nod.

"The baby is Milo's."

"Oh, God, Kai..."

"Truth or lie?"

"Truth?"

I shrug because I don't know.

"Truth or lie, the baby is Enzo's," I say.

"Please, let that be the truth."

Again, I shrug. Both men fucked me the same night, well Milo raped me ,and Enzo fucked me, but the result could be the same.

"What are you going to do? Are you going to be able to carry the baby if it's Milo's?"

I shrug—because I don't know. This baby will be an heir to a dangerous empire. The baby will be my heir. But the child could also be Enzo's or Milo's heir.

If the baby is Milo's heir, then Felix, the child's uncle, could try to influence his or her decisions. Felix would want to raise the child in hopes of gaining control over the Black empire.

But it could be worse if it is Enzo's child. *Not for me.* I would love to have Enzo's child, but because of what Milo told me.

.

.

.

"You think you and Enzo are the first two to fall in love while playing to become the king?" Milo laughs.

My eyes widen.

"Every few generations, a woman and a man go head to head, the last time it happened was the worst. They had a child together, got married, and said they would rule together. But the entire organization requires only one person to lead—the strongest. And the competition gives the men faith the strongest will lead them into the worst battles. It gives them faith they will win against any enemy. And so when the competitors fell in love with each other and produced a child who would have no challenger to the throne, potentially growing into a weak, vulnerable leader, the men revolted. They started killing friends and family members the couple loved.

"One by one, the couple watched those they loved die. Each time it shattered their love a little more. Ten people died, but it wasn't enough to break their love, until they had a child. And that child was killed."

Fuck.

"So you see, I'm helping you by stealing the love you feel for Enzo from you. You will be so tortured and pained you won't be able to love him without some serious healing. But you know you won't deep down. Because the same thing will happen to you. You will never put those you love at risk just so you can love Enzo again. Let me break you. Let me take that love with me when I leave you."

.

.

.

I grab my stomach. This baby is at risk, and he or she isn't even born yet. I won't let a child be born into this world. I won't let my child fight in some twisted game. I won't let my child be used as a pawn by Felix. I won't let my child come between Enzo and me.

Liesel watches me as I let the truth of the situation pass over me. But I don't tell her the truth. She can see it on my face though, and she knows the torment I've been dealing with and the burden I carry.

"Truth or lie? I have a child," Liesel says.

My eyes shoot to her, and I know immediately she speaks the truth. "Truth."

She nods.

But I can't open my mouth to ask the question that will burn with me until I know the answer. Is Enzo her child's father?

Liesel will tell me if she wants to. It's none of my business. So I ask a helpful question instead.

"How did you hide it from Enzo?" Because if I decide to keep this baby growing inside me, then the child will never be safe unless I hide it.

"By giving him up," she says through tears.

We sit in silence for a moment as we both cry quietly.

"Truth or lie, I don't love Enzo Black," I say.

"Lie," Enzo says, and I jump.

I don't know how he got through the locked door, but he's standing watching the two of us with confusion on his face. He clearly didn't hear the earlier part of our conversation.

"Truth," I say, breaking his heart.

And for the first time since I fell for Enzo, I'm speaking

the truth. I don't love Enzo. Milo twisted my feelings. He stole my love. And my unborn child filled that void.

With hard work and time, I could get Enzo's love back. But in this fucked up world we were born into, I can't love them both and keep them both alive. So I know I will never try to get the love I feel for Enzo back. I'll choose not to heal. And in doing so, I will keep my baby, and Enzo, safe.

The End

Thank you so much for reading! Kai and Enzo's story continues in Possessed by Lies!

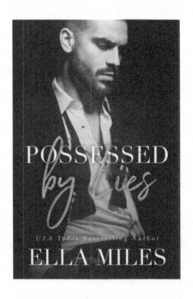

FREE BOOKS

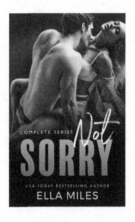

Read **Not Sorry** for **FREE!** And sign up to get my latest releases, updates, and more goodies here→EllaMiles.com/freebooks

Follow me on BookBub to get notified of my new releases and recommendations here→Follow on BookBub Here

Join Ella's Bellas FB group for giveaways and FUN & a
FREE copy of **Pretend I'm Yours**→Join Ella's Bellas Here

ALSO BY ELLA MILES

TRUTH OR LIES (Coming 2019):

Lured by Lies #0.5

Taken by Lies #1

Betrayed by Truths #2

Trapped by Lies #3

Stolen by Truths #4

Possessed by Lies #5

Consumed by Truths #6

DIRTY SERIES:

Dirty Beginning

Dirty Obsession

Dirty Addiction

Dirty Revenge

Dirty: The Complete Series

ALIGNED SERIES:

Aligned: Volume 1 (Free Series Starter)

Aligned: Volume 2

Aligned: Volume 3

Aligned: Volume 4

Aligned: The Complete Series Boxset

UNFORGIVABLE SERIES:

Heart of a Thief

Heart of a Liar

Heart of a Prick

Unforgivable: The Complete Series Boxset

MAYBE, DEFINITELY SERIES:

Maybe Yes

Maybe Never

Maybe Always

Definitely Yes

Definitely No

Definitely Forever

STANDALONES:

Pretend I'm Yours

Finding Perfect

Savage Love

Too Much

Not Sorry

ABOUT THE AUTHOR

Ella Miles writes steamy romance, including everything from dark suspense romance that will leave you on the edge of your seat to contemporary romance that will leave you laughing out loud or crying. Most importantly, she wants you to feel everything her characters feel as you read.

Ella is currently living her own happily ever after near the Rocky Mountains with her high school sweetheart husband. Her heart is also taken by her goofy five year old black lab who is scared of everything, including her own shadow.

Ella is a USA Today Bestselling Author & Top 50 Bestselling Author.

Stalk Ella at:
www.ellamiles.com
ella@ellamiles.com